WHAT IS THE POWER
OF BITHE?

We have no records, only legends. Some say that few Old Ones survived. Those who loved us rose up and destroyed those who enslaved us. But the legends do not say that *all* who enslaved us died.

There lies our fear. If those who hated us have lived all these years in some secret place, and they have now chosen to return . . .

What is this power that suddenly drives our people to war against each other?

Who is this Bithe? Is he an Old One? Or perhaps, more dangerously, an offworlder?

Books by Max Daniels

Offworld
The Space Guardian

Published by POCKET BOOKS

Max Daniels

OFFWORLD

PUBLISHED BY POCKET BOOKS NEW YORK

Another *Original* publication of POCKET BOOKS

POCKET BOOKS, a Simon & Schuster division of
GULF & WESTERN CORPORATION
1230 Avenue of the Americas, New York, N.Y. 10020

ISBN: 0-671-81887-2

First Pocket Books printing February, 1979

Trademarks registered in the United States and other countries.

Printed in the U.S.A.

OFFWORLD.

Chapter 1

In the featureless room in which Max sat on a cot, there was nothing to look at, nothing to do. The only item in the room besides the cot was the button that would summon an Officer of the Court. He had only to push that button and all his problems and conflicts would be solved. Of course, he wouldn't be Max anymore either. He would walk like Max and talk like Max—but he sure as hell wouldn't think like Max.

What was incomprehensible to Max was why the results of his thinking processes always turned out to be an offense to society. He didn't object to his society. He thought it good, excellent, almost ideal. He was a history buff and knew what horrors this present society had developed from. It was a good, fair, just society. It took into account all the worst features of *Homo sapiens'* psyche and provided outlets. It—it—it was damned dull! Even so, it was his own fault that he was a rebel when there was nothing to rebel against. He was too aggressive in the wrong ways—and his sense of humor was definitely warped way out of line.

A short crack of laughter burst from Max as he remembered the prank that had precipitated him into this situation. He still thought it was funny. No one had been hurt; no one had lost a single credit by it. True, he had robbed a bank, but he had sent back every single credit. After all, it wasn't his fault that they had been idiots enough to soak the box with the money just because they heard the clock ticking inside and he had labeled it BOMB—HANDLE WITH CAUTION. Who the hell would send a bomb carefully labeled?

Maybe what rankled was that the Director of the bank had gotten a wad of wet credits in the face. It had made a funny item in the news—and if the Director had not been a publicity hound and had not insisted on being the one to open the package, the whole world would not have been entertained by his discomfiture. The wetting had not interfered with the violent expulsion of the money. The device was mechanical, of course. Max would not take a chance on even a mild explosive. He had no desire at all to hurt anyone.

It had merely occurred to him one day while he was in the bank how easy it would be to rob the place—so he had. Perhaps he should not have sent that letter outlining the procedure he had used to the newscasters, but it seemed the simplest and most direct way of getting an immediate tightening of the breach in security he had noticed.

No matter how Max twisted and turned what he had done and what had later been said about it, he could not feel he had been wrong. In fact, he had accomplished a great deal of good. He had provided the banks with greater security. He had thereby prevented someone with less altruistic intentions from defrauding society and, possibly, even injuring a bank employee. He had deflated a pompous Director (although that was serendipitous, Max had to admit). He had provided the newscasters with a good story and the public with much amusement and something to talk about. Why was everyone so angry with him?

Of course, there had been other incidents too. That time he had pointed out a hazard to the water supply of the city by dropping in a dye. It had been a completely harmless dye, colorless until it passed through the body. But some people had been badly frightened when they urinated bright blue. Perhaps that time he had gone a little too far. And the time that . . .

Well, maybe it was not only the bank robbery. As Max thought back, there did seem to be an awful lot of pranks. All of them had been harmless, all had accomplished a good purpose, but they had created a good deal of turmoil. Was turmoil enough reason to send a man, disintegrated into atoms, through space to an unimaginably distant world where he was supposed to reintegrate? And did the Transporter really transport, or was it a euphemism for execution?

That thought, passing through Max's mind periodically, had given him pause. He knew there was nothing wrong with noticing the weaknesses of society. In fact, each time he had been censured for his pranks he had been praised for seeing what others missed. If he pushed that button and permitted them to readjust his personality, they would not take away his ability to notice—only his desire to make people laugh at what he had seen. In fact, they would make him into a pompous prig.

Max rose, proving himself to be yet another example of the exquisite result of a thorough mixing of the races on his planet. He was 1.8 meters in height and weighed 80 kilos. His body was heavily muscled under a warm brown skin. Straight black hair, coarse and shining but cut short for professional purposes, dipped into a deep peak on his forehead and emphasized the slant of the large dark eyes that came with his color from his Negro ancestry. The epicanthic fold, betraying the Mongolian strain, was prominent, as were the flat, high cheekbones, but the nose and thin but shapely lips were pure Caucasian.

With lithe grace Max began to pace his confined quarters restlessly. He stopped short when he noticed that each circuit was bringing him closer and closer to that button. It glared at him, bright red against the soft gray walls. Was his choice between the cessation of laughter and the cessation of life?

That red button was hypnotic. Such a bright, cheerful color. Red for life, dull gray for oblivion? And what would he do with that life? Max's hand, which had started to move upward, dropped. He would go on teaching little boys and girls the basics of armed and unarmed combat and grown men and women the fine points of the same. There was nothing wrong with his job; it was necessary and important. The wrestling, savate, karate, judo, kung fu, aikido, the use of the rapier, saber, and épée were the key to world peace. All men and women were trained to fight and encouraged to do so regularly as an outlet for their aggressions. Government officials were required by law to do three sessions a day with a Master. When Max stopped to think about it, he realized he had probably saved the world much trouble and grief by working over Mr. Secretary or Madame President.

There was some satisfaction in that, but not enough. Turning away from that beguiling red button, Max began to pace again. Was there a real desire for violence in him? He was always reading history, thrilled and excited by what he knew should horrify him. Why, every so often he found himself wishing he had lived in the days of the Terror—and that was pure idiocy. Had he lived then, he probably would not have lived long. Ninety percent of the people had died, one way or another, in the Terror. But for him, life was a little too guaranteed these days. The training in personal combat was coupled with strong taboos against actual injury to a combat partner. In fact, those psychotic individuals who killed deliberately were executed. That train of thought stopped Max in his tracks.

There were executions. They were public, and no silly platitudes about retribution or punishment were mouthed. Those who killed deliberately outside of the conditions set for a formal duel were a danger to society and were removed from it as quickly as they could be caught and their guilt established. And no euphemism was applied; an execution was called an execution.

Max's spirits rose. He knew that space travel had been achieved. Against all laws of military logistics, Earth had once been invaded by aliens. The Nompeg were attracted by the enormous population, in which they saw an endless supply of slaves and meat for the table, and by the constant wars, which they felt would prevent the planet from unifying against them. In that they had been wrong. Like the members of a squabbling family, Earthmen had quickly sunk

11

their differences to fight together against the attack by
outsiders. Under pressure of need, space travel had
been perfected so that when the Nompeg had been
defeated they could be pursued to their own planet.
That planet and all its colonies had been ruthlessly
destroyed. But only a hundredth of the teeming bil-
lions of men survived the Terror, and the loathsome
form and aims of the Nompeg were branded on men's
minds.

However tragic, the Terror had actually been of
enormous benefit, producing a unified planet with an
easily manageable population. Before the memory of
what had attracted the Nompeg could fade, restric-
tive breeding laws were passed. Then the need for
raw materials diminished with the perfection of re-
cycling techniques, and the energy problem was
solved by the switch to solar energy and a hydro-
gen economy. Space travel had been abandoned.
There was no need to mine the uninhabitable planets
of the system, no population pressure to make terra-
forming worthwhile, and travel to the stars, when
fear and hatred were no longer driving forces, simply
took too long.

Man's inquisitive mind still delved into the mys-
teries of the universe. Fusion power was available
—power enough to move the planet, to warm it if the
sun died. Why not power enough to send a man
through a space–time warp? Max was a history buff, not
especially interested in science. It was not unlikely he
had missed published information about the Transporter. Max's spirits rose still further. He suddenly remembered that the Judicial Councillor had not really
been angry.

That was why the sentence had been such a shock.
The police judge had been furious, castigating Max

for his antisocial behavior and his infantile sense of humor. Finally, when Max just grinned, he had slammed the dossier closed and remanded Max's case to a Judicial Councillor. Then Max had felt his first twinge of apprehension. But the Councillor had been a woman of another stamp. The black-robed figure sat quietly, only her eyes moving, flicking from Max's records to Max himself. The only other movements she had made were when she turned a page and when her lips twitched in suppressed mirth. And then she had closed the folder and spoken one sentence.

"Transportation or personality adjustment."

Max felt the shock all over again now. His heart checked, then began to pound. But even in the isolation of the Consideration Chamber, he reacted in the same way. His head came up proudly and his broad shoulders went back. And then the click of the door latch startled him, because he was buried in thought, so that his hands came up in defensive combat position.

The Judicial Councillor stood still. In automatic response to the combat-raised hands, hers clasped behind her back in rejection. Max's hands dropped. "You have not summoned an Integration Officer for discussion or explanation. I must assume you have formally chosen Transportation," the Councillor said gently.

There was no disapproval in her voice. In fact, Max was surprised to detect the faintest glimmer of admiration, perhaps even reminiscent longing in her expression. His heart leaped again. Transportation was real; it must be real. Soon, soon, he would be free. There would be a whole new world—a *new* world.

13

"Yes."

"Please read this statement and thumbprint it."

The sheet contained only a few sentences to the effect that Max had been given time to consider and had chosen to be Transported. He pressed his thumb to the sensitized corner of the sheet. That was all. There was no ceremony, no sentence, no lecture. Somehow that made it much more awful. Only the Councillor accompanied him down the silent corridor. She spoke only once, to inform him that signing the release was not irrevocable. He could change his mind and opt for personality change at any moment up until the Transporter switch was pulled. He need only call out.

At a door no different from any other in the corridor, the Councillor stopped. After the smallest of hesitations, Max opened the door. He was very frightened, but a strong feeling of resentment was building up in him. It seemed unfair that, after you had made such a hard choice, you should not have a little help. It was cruel to say the release was not irrevocable. You had to make the same horrible decision over and over every single second until the switch went down. The Councillor had not even said "Goodbye" or "Good luck." That was cruel two ways—implying that you would change your mind and—and it was lonely.

A large printed notice that Max had been staring at unseeingly finally impinged on his brain.

REMOVE ALL CLOTHING

At first Max started to walk around the panel on which the notice was printed without complying, but then his sense of humor was touched. Naked he had come into the world, and naked he would go out of it —if that was what the stupid rules were.

14

It was only after he started to undress that he saw the smaller print underneath.

Only living organic tissue is perfectly reintegrated. Inanimate materials may be reintegrated incorrectly with or within living tissue, causing injury or death.

Max was first terrified when he realized how close his rebelliousness had brought him to an agonizing death. Then his resentment increased. The notice could have read DANGER—REMOVE CLOTHING, or something similar, so that one would not think it was just spitefulness, wanting to send a misfit naked into a new world. But as he slipped off his shoes, Max suddenly grinned with pleasure.

It worked. It really worked. They must have some way of seeing where you went and what happened. Max paused, bent over, removing his second shoe, as a rather startling idea struck him. Could there be some purpose to Transporting him? There was no evidence at all for such a wild notion. All he had been told about Transportation was that it was permanent and that the world he would be deposited upon would be livable; that is, most animals and plants would be edible, the air would be breathable, and some areas would have suitable temperature ranges.

Not by the slightest innuendo had Max been led to believe that the world was deliberately chosen. Only his society had a centuries-long habit of not wasting a tittle or a jot of anything. Even the dead were recycled. Would they throw away a live man? But no smallest hint of what he was supposed to do had been given. Nonetheless, Max pushed off his shoe and stripped off his briefs eagerly, stepped around the instruction panel, and hurried to the tall black cylinder that stood alone in the center of the room.

Here he stopped dead. However, this was no new change of mood. ENTER HERE the cylinder said, but it seemed as blank and featureless as a perfect ball bearing. Max felt around, wondering whether he had missed seeing a latch because of the impenetrable blackness of the material. Under his fingers the cylinder was as smooth as it looked.

"God damn it," Max snarled under his breath, "if this is a stubbornness contest to see if I'll give up in frustration, I know who's going to win."

Furious, he circled once, twice, feeling and probing with no result. Finally, setting his jaw, he walked straight at the ENTER HERE sign.

Blackness engulfed him. Blackness was the wrong word. There had never been anything as black as this black. That was the first thought that flashed through Max's mind. The second was briefer—a flicker of amusement at the literal-mindedness of whoever designed those signs. ENTER HERE, indeed! The third had barely begun—malicious satisfaction in traversing the last step in an obstacle course designed to discourage the fainthearted and doubtful—when a cold as intense as the blackness settled on him.

Max had not even time to gasp before a pain so pervasive and so intense gripped him that he screamed—only there was no sound. He was burning, every cell, every atom was individually on fire. Scream after scream echoed in his mind, bursting silently into nothing. Bursting! Bursting! And then his brain itself burst—and there was nothing.

Chapter 2

What the hell had gotten into the sheets, Max wondered as he shifted slightly to avoid the prickles. And, almost simultaneously with the thought, he remembered. The memory of pain was eased by a thrill of relief. He was alive; he was Max; he was free of the constrictive taboos of his overcivilized world.

Slowly he raised his lids and a gasp of pleasure was drawn from him. His eyes had opened on a most exquisite pale lavender sky. He sat up abruptly, a smooth, fluid movement that assured him his body was unharmed and in perfect condition. His second view of his new world was not quite so inviting. As far as he could see in every direction, a flat and featureless plain extended.

What leaped immediately to Max's mind was essential—food and water. His appetitie had not been of the best since his sentencing, and the first reaction of his body to his emotional relief was hunger and thirst. Naturally enough the desire was intensified as soon as Max realized that neither food nor water was immediately available. Max passed his tongue over his lips to wet them and instantly became aware that his back was damp. But the earth under his fingers was dry, and the lavender sky was cloudless. Max turned his attention to the growth upon which he was sitting. It was a dark reddish brown, not very attractive but somehow familiar. The stems were thick and leathery; the leaves, if they were leaves, were bulbous knobs. Experimentally Max squeezed a bulb. It burst at once, releasing a few drops of clear liquid.

The action brought to mind the familiar plant—a seaweed. Only in the seaweed the bulbs had been filled with air. Air in an ocean environment. Water in a desert? Max's back was now dry. He wriggled it experimentally. It did not feel especially sticky, which meant, perhaps, that there was not a high concentration of plant chemicals in the fluid. Max glanced around again at the featureless plain, shrugged his shoulders, and popped a bulb into his mouth.

There was a very faintly sweet taste, reminiscent of the effect of chewing a blade of grass. Max hesitated, then shrugged again and popped four or five more bulbs with his teeth. That was about a teaspoon of liquid, not enough—unless it contained a very virulent poison—to do more than make him slightly sick. In a few hours he would know whether he had a drinking supply or not. If the liquid were wholesome, Max thought, he would try chewing the stems and leaves. Certain types of seaweed were considered a delicacy on his home planet. The idea of being set down in a kilometers-wide field of "delicacy" made Max grin, and the touch of humor increased his confidence.

Somehow he was sure his people knew where he had been sent, and, obviously, it would have to be to an uninhabited area. The arrival of a naked man out of thin air in a town or village would not be conducive to calm acceptance. He turned slowly, shading his eyes from the glare of the pale green sun. There, distant but clear, was a darker line on the horizon—trees or hills. Trees meant water and a stick for a weapon; hills meant streams and rocks for throwing.

The green sun was warm and the breeze was cool—an ideal day for a long hike. The spongy growth was soft to walk on, and the moisture released by crushing the bulbs cooled the feet. By the time the sun had moved appreciably in the direction Max called west—although he knew that it might just as easily be north, south, or east—Max knew he could survive, and by the afternoon of his second day on his new world he had developed a strong affection for the unattractive-looking water weed.

The plant seemed able to provide an answer to any problem. Inspired by his inability to chew some of the fibers, Max fell to knotting together the flattened bulbs of his last drink. They had even more tensile strength than he expected and he soon had a substantial belt. Into this he began to hook main stems. By evening Max had a primitive kilt. He was rather surprised when it held together after he fastened it around his narrow hips, and he was even more surprised at the sense of confidence it gave him. Max wondered whether nudity was alien to his species or whether some garment—at least to protect the pubic area—had been worn for so long that the need was akin to a racial memory.

That night Max lay flat, looking to the "east,"

watching the sky darken into a magnificent royal purple. What surprised him most was his lack of regret. In spite of moments of despair and terror, not once had he been sorry about the choice he had made. He, urban bred, had not for a moment missed the crush of humanity. It was true he was looking forward to meeting the inhabitants of this world, but that was because —because—

As Max's eyes closed, he was dimly aware that his desire to meet the people was not mere curiosity. The sooner he met them, the sooner he could begin to— begin to— He slept, knowing in his dreams what it was he had to do, horrified, but frantic with the urgency of his task. The wild sense of need brought him wide awake and onto his feet before he realized he had been dreaming, and the shock wiped out the actual substance of the dream.

For a while Max lay awake trying to remember and watching the moons. Six were now showing. Three were a greenish silver, which seemed right if they were reflecting the greenish sun. But two were, unaccountably, a bright red. The sixth, a silvery pink, hung somewhat below and almost perfectly midway between them, giving the impression of two glaring red eyes above an open, greedy mouth. Those three were quite a puzzle. Wondering about them was soothing, and Max drifted off to sleep again.

Morning brought a pleasant surprise and a disappointment. In the pale greenish light of dawn, Max could see that he was closer than he expected to his goal, but the goal itself was less attractive than his expectations. Instead of the forest or wooded area he had hoped for, Max was facing a long, slow rise studded with low brush. Beyond—what he had really seen—were towering mountains, their tops white with snow that mirrored the lavender sky and disappeared into it. Nowhere did he see the shining threads that betrayed a surface stream.

Max breakfasted (as he had breakfasted, lunched, and dined each day before) on water weed, chewing ruminatively while he walked, his mind busy with the deep defiles he could see in the mountains and the perfectly flat plain. From vague memories of a smattering of geology he thought these were signs of a very old planet. Had civilizations risen and fallen? How did he know the people he would meet would be technologically backward? His pace did not falter, but he remembered suddenly he had had an important revelation in a dream—only he couldn't remember what it was. That made him laugh aloud, but the laughter cut off sharply. There had been nothing funny about the dream.

It was not that Max believed in dreams. Dreams, he knew, were the integration of experience into memory patterns—the subconscious sorting and storage mechanism of the most complex computer that had ever existed—the intelligent brain. But that sorting and storage could be influenced by many things besides experience. Certain drugs could disorient it completely. And hypnotic suggestion could alter, twist, or channel that sorting.

Max's lips tightened over his teeth as urgency stung him again. Okay, okay, he told the nagging sensation of purpose, I'm going as fast as I can. He was sure now that a task with a large purpose had been suggested to him, although he did not know what the purpose was. He had been used. Possibly the bank business had been a setup; perhaps the lack of security had been arranged at the bank with which he dealt because the government knew he would react, and even how he would react, but Max felt no resentment. His people were merely giving him what he wanted. All his life he had lacked a sense of large purpose as contrasted with small accomplishments, no matter how excellent.

Not for him, Max knew, was the polishing of an already well-cut jewel into perfection. He craved the violent hacking out of the raw gems—the sudden exhilaration of seizing what seemed to be a pebble of dross and seeing in it the jewel of the future. His legs, warmed out of their aching stiffness, drove smoothly onward. I am going as fast as I can, he assured himself joyfully as a delicious sense of anticipation overrode the lingering impression of horror his dream had left.

As long as he could not see any definite signs of water, Max knew he could not abandon the water weed. It did not stop abruptly but grew more and more sparsely. Between the water weed clumps were patches of tough dry grass, its sere pale brown touched with red, and bare arid soil. This did not have the uniformly fine consistency Max had found under the water weed. Pebbles were plentiful, and here and there a rock appeared. Max's feet were somewhat less enthusiastic about this phenomenon than his brain, and he uttered a short yelp as he trod on a sharp stone.

Nonetheless, rocks were useful things. If he could find three fairly round, of about the same size, he could make a bola. It was not a weapon with which he had much experience, but he knew the principles of its construction and use from his study of historical weapons. Theoretically, if he found the right sort of rocks, he would soon also be able to chip a knife and spear for himself (provided he ever found a tree large enough to make a shaft). What was more, he could have a fire.

Max's pace slowed as he examined every rock he passed. He chose two of seemingly the same composition and struck them sharply together. No chips, no sparks. He dropped one, chose another of seemingly different composition. Again neither chips nor sparks. With only an occasional glance to be sure he was not wandering too far from the water weed, Max continued his experiments. He did not solve his problems immediately, but he was successful enough to make his search of absorbing interest. By the time the green sun was just above the mountain tops, he had two rocks for his bola tied together with water weed and slung around his neck and he had a pair of rocks that emitted a very faint spark when struck together.

He was hoping to find the third bola rock and a better piece of flint before sundown. Most small animals came out to feed at sundown, and Max hoped to catch dinner, because he had seen an occasional hole under a grass tussock. The flint was necessary too. Max felt almost hungry enough for meat to eat it raw, but not quite. His eyes fixed on the ground, Max moved in an erratic zigzag until an enormous hiss—a hiss that could have been emitted by the great-grandfather of all serpents—froze him in his tracks.

Quicker than thought, the rocks on their leash were over his head and whirling in the air as Max spun to face the sound. His eyes caught movement; the rocks flew toward it. A fast side kick toward a second, peripherally perceived shadow demolished it; his hands connected with a third.

Max hesitated, knees slightly flexed to propel him in any direction, hands up at combat ready in warning. A flicker in the air— Max's hand flickered faster. A spear caught in flight was reversed, readied. A single human-sounding shout froze all action again.

Now Max's brain had time to catch up with his reflexes. On the ground lay three—men? At a little distance five others sat astride—dinosaurs? Movement on the ground. Max leaped toward the being the rocks had felled, his newly acquired spear pointed suggestively toward the throat. The other two, Max knew, would not move so soon. He watched the mounted beings.

One, who had been a little in advance of the others, urged his mount a step forward. Max moved his spear until it touched the throat of the fallen person. The being astride reined his beast back. Max sighed with relief. His bluff had worked. He knew that even to save his own life he could not have pushed that spear home. The mounted being called something aloud. Since the person under the spear did not answer, Max assumed the remark was addressed to him.

"I can't understand you," he replied.

Another sentence was spoken at him, more hesitantly, as if the being were using a language with which he was not completely familiar. Max shook his head.

"It doesn't matter if you can speak nine thousand nine hundred and seventy-three dialects," he said, grinning. "You aren't going to find one I know."

The grin had more effect than any other exchange could. The person who had spoken handed his reins to another beside him, then handed over his spear. Ostentatiously he began to divest himself of his other weapons. Another being said something sharply and there was an exchange that Max judged from the tone to be an argument. He also assumed from the gestures that the argument concerned the two unconscious beings, and his eyes flicked toward them in sudden anxiety.

Men of his own species could not have been seriously injured by the blows Max had dealt, but these people were emphatically not of his own species. Max's breath caught as his conditioned fear of maiming and killing caught at him. He shouted, "Hey!" and with his free hand beckoned impatiently and pointed to the still forms.

His voice and gesture stilled the argument. The now weaponless person who had addressed him first looked puzzled and then, when Max stepped back a little from the being he was threatening and motioned again, dismounted. He came forward, slowly at first and then more quickly as Max made no further threatening gesture, holding his empty hands palm up toward Max. Max nodded encouragingly, hoping the motion meant the same thing here as at home. Apparently it did, but the basic intention was in doubt. When he came to his fallen companions, the being looked down and then started toward Max again.

"No," Max said firmly, shaking his head and pointing again at the quiet bodies.

The being looked back at the still forms, but now Max did not know how to explain that he wanted to know whether they were alive. Just as he was considering some elaborate playacting that might have gotten him into trouble, one of the prone forms twitched. Almost simultaneously, the other groaned. Sighing with relief, Max grinned again and nodded happily. He stepped back still further and lifted his spear away from the person he had been threatening.

An excited babble broke out among the mounted beings. The one who had been arguing with the leader, who was now staring somewhat bemusedly at his reviving companions, leaped down from his mount and ran to help the groaning one sit upright. Cautiously, Max lifted the spear he held to a nonoffensive position. The unarmed man stepped forward again, voicing an eager question and pointing at the two on the ground and then to Max's hands and feet.

"I'd love to," Max replied smilingly, "only I don't know what the hell you're saying. Do you want me to lay you out too or show you how?"

He knew that what he said was not important. What was essential was the smile, mirrored on the face looking at him, and the tone of his voice. Max slipped the spear he had caught into the crook of his arm and held out his hands also. His left elbow was promptly gripped, the left elbow of the leader presented suggestively to his right hand.

Somewhere in the back of his mind Max was aware of hoping he was not admitting defeat or selling himself into slavery, but his overriding emotion was one of shock. The hand that touched him was as warm as his own, and the elbow he gripped was as smooth as his own skin. It was the last thing he expected, for the beings he faced were covered with what looked like the silvery scales of fish or reptiles.

They were, Max decided, as his elbow was released, an exquisitely beautiful race by human standards, and they were completely humanoid except for the scales and the coloring. They were silver all over. The silver hair, if it was hair, was dressed as in pictures Max remembered of American Indians—parted in the center and hanging in two heavy plaits over each shoulder. The eyes were silver too, darker for the iris, the black slit pupil the only break in the color scheme. The lips were ebony black and gleaming as was the inside of the mouth, against which the white teeth were startling.

Now the being who had been groaning was helped to its feet and Max saw to his chagrin that it was female. She was holding what would have been the solar plexus in *Homo sapiens* and breathing very carefully. Nonetheless, she made her way determinedly forward. Max watched her faltering progress cautiously, but a right hand was extended eagerly toward Max's left elbow and Max repeated the gripping ceremony.

A gentle touch on his right arm brought Max's left hand up for a chop. Fortunately, he saw his two-thirds of a bola being extended toward him at arm's length and checked the blow. As he hung the weapon around his neck, a new spate of questioning broke out. Max pointed to the two rocks and held up the third empty water weed leash, shaking his head. He hoped they would understand that the weapon was incomplete and not think he was refusing to show how it worked. In fact, he was awfully glad it was incomplete. It was a pure fluke that he had managed to tangle his attacker in it.

There was another round of arm gripping, but now Max moved. The one who had been twitching had not yet fully revived, and Max pushed gently but insistently toward him. A tense silence fell as Max knelt beside his erstwhile opponent. Deliberately, he laid aside his spear. Max was concerned about the being he had felled, but he also wished to test his new "friends." If they were of a treacherous nature, he was offering them a seemingly perfect opportunity to kill him or turn the tables on him.

Gently, he lifted his victim's eyelids. The pupils were the same size and Max could only hope that the significance was the same as for his own species. Then he slipped his hand behind the being's neck to feel the vertebrae. They were certainly different from his own, Max thought, but there did not seem to be anything broken. He slid his hand under the heavy hair to pinch an earlobe and drew breath—no ears.

The being muttered something, and Max looked questioningly at the group now surrounding him. Incidentally, he noted that the spear had not been moved. His first contact shook his head negatively. The mutter probably had no meaning. Max moved his victim's head slowly from side to side. That brought a sharp exclamation and a hand lifted waveringly toward an aching neck. That was better. Max smiled and began to massage neck and shoulder with practiced fingers. Soon the person sat up, muttering more purposefully words that made the leader of the party laugh. There was another spate of babble— apparently explanations—and another elbow gripping ceremony.

As Max's last victim picked himself up, the leader looked at Max in a troubled way. Finally, he made a wide gesture that encompassed his whole group, pointed to the mounts, and then pointed away in the general direction Max had been going. Then he pointed to Max and let his hands drop. Although Max was not sure whether his new friend was asking where he was going, expressing an invitation, or indicating that he was sorry there was no extra mount, he did not care.

"That's okay," Max replied, accompanying the words with pointing at himself and then firmly in the same direction. "I'm going your way—whatever way you're going—and I'll be glad to walk," he added, casting a jaundiced eye on the mounts the group was using.

A relieved smile broke out on all faces. Max's captured spear was picked up and thrust into his hand, and, after a gesture Max interpreted as an invitation for him to accompany them, the group turned toward their mounts. The closer Max got, the less enthusiastic he—became. From a distance the beasts had reminded him of something unpleasant he had seen in entertainment films. As he drew nearer he suddenly remembered what they looked like. Who wanted to ride a small (and not that small, all things considered) version of *Tyrannosaurus rex?*

It was apparent, however, that he was not going to have a choice. The group leader was unstrapping a cloak or blanket of blackish, supple hide, folding it, and fastening it behind the saddle of one of the beasts. Max looked at the thing and repressed a shudder. Each of its three toes was as big as his hand and was fitted with a claw of appropriate size. At the thigh, the leg was as massive as his own shoulders. The set of the body was less upright than that of *rex,* the back sufficiently horizontal so that a saddle, fastened forward under the forearms and behind under the massive tail, would perch with only a slight tilt. What made Max particularly uneasy was the fact that the saddle buckle was well within reach of the nasty little four-fingered hands. Max preferred not to look at the head at all. It was true that the teeth were a mere six centimeters long rather than twelve, but they still looked capable of extracting a substantial bite from anything the creature decided was tasty.

Later, Max found he had done the larths a grave injustice. Although the wild variety could, and not infrequently did, tear people apart, the domesticated creatures were far better tempered than they looked. In fact, raised from the egg by pevi (people), they were touchingly affectionate and loyal and had been known to starve to death rather than attack a live master or even eat a dead one. This latter stupidity was also characteristic—the larths were by no means bright. A very ancient definition of the horse—a nervous and unintelligent animal—applied to them very well.

To delay mounting, even by moments, Max drew the leader's attention, pointed to himself, and said, "Max." The pevi, fortunately, were a good deal more intelligent than their beasts. In immediate response, the leader touched himself and said "Xers." He then pointed in turn to the two males and the female Max had gripped elbows with. "Labin, Chelv, Arile." Smiling, he pointed at the beast. "Larth." And then, very slowly and clearly he added, *"Max wimbril larth mer Arile."*

The moment of truth had come, but it was less excruciating than Max had expected because he was so busy with the implications of what he had heard—more than heard: understood. If the language was analytic rather than synthetic, what Xers had said was, "Max will ride the larth with Arile." Soon language lessons would really begin and real communication could be established.

Chapter 3

At first Max was amazed at the rapidity with which he learned the new language. He had studied languages previously—some to enable him to communicate with important clients, others to facilitate his historical hobby. But even though he was accustomed to absorbing new grammar and vocabulary, his progress in Enthok was phenomenal. When he stopped to think, his surprise diminished. This vocabulary was constantly reinforced by use. He had no time to forget a new word because it was used so frequently. On the other hand, all the other languages he knew were suppressed because there was never any occasion to use them. Within a week—that is, ten days new planet time— he was thinking and dreaming in Enthok.

On arrival at their destination, Max was immediately aware that he had joined a group that had just suffered a catastrophe. It was not only that the camp was carefully arranged and patrolled—that might be a result of a continuous state of raiding. More significant was the fact that about two-thirds of the adults in the camp were wounded and the number of children seemed disproportionate. Not knowing at first how low the birthrate was, Max did not fully appreciate the magnitude of the disaster.

Moreover, many of the children, although they did not cry, looked stunned and grief-stricken. They seemed to be seeking what they knew they would never find, wandering restlessly from tent to tent, although they were welcomed and caressed with infinite tenderness by any adult they approached. It did not require divination to understand that those poor creatures had been recently orphaned. The fact that they were so tenderly treated together with the gentle firmness exhibited toward the domestic animals in the camp, the care lavished on the wounded—even those who would never fight again—and the warm courtesy extended to himself made Max determine to join this group if they would accept him.

In fact, from every angle Max examined them, the Pevi Vinci Enthok (warriors, people, citizens of Clan Vinci of the tribe of Enthok) seemed admirable. They were an undegenerate fighting culture; that is, they loved fighting, practiced its arts, and engaged in it frequently without really desiring the results of fighting —the power and the domination of the victor. Nor had the warring yet blunted their sensibilities or brutalized them. Thus far, the clan was balancing harmony at home with external aggression.

"Pev Max?"

Max raised a hand, palm forward, in standard greeting. "Zel Xers," he replied, "Come in. Be seated. How can I make you welcome?"

He did not rise. Although he had addressed Xers by his title, which conveyed a mixture of tribal leader, battle captain, and ruler, no courtesies other than common politeness were expected. The Enthok seemed to be far enough from the primitive to have shed most senseless superstitious taboos regarding speech and behavior and not yet "civilized" enough to have replaced that form of idiocy with the greater idiocy of "manners." Their living patterns at this stage were sensible, convenient, and considerate.

In fact, the society was totally nonsexist and classless. Max found it fascinating that there were no distinguishing pronouns for he or she. The universal *"re"* applied to both sexes and *"rels"* to the possessive. Moreover, males and females performed all tasks —fighting, hunting, child rearing, cooking, and household chores—indiscriminately. Probably that was a direct result of the reptilian ancestry. The females laid a single medium-sized, flexible-skinned egg. The process did not inconvenience them at all and the egg needed little care beyond moderate warmth.

"I have eaten. I have drunk. I have slept," Xers replied formally to Max's formal question as he seated himself. Then he broke into a smile. "You speak our language well now. You have even learned our ways."

"Because they are good ways, it is easy to learn them," Max responded sincerely.

Xers did not reply directly to Max's compliment. Instead he said, "It's time, Pev Max, for us to talk of your past and your future." Then an apologetic note crept into his voice. "Forgive me for speaking so plainly. Please believe that you are welcome to our tents, to our fire, and to our table as long as you desire, but we ourselves must soon come to a great decision. We must know what is your purpose so that we may

33

part in amity before secrets are told or you may decide to share our fate."

Max's face lit with enthusiasm. "I am very glad. I am pev [an adult] not briska [an infant] and I have felt myself to be a useless burden. It is time, indeed, that I begin to earn my food, or thank you for your hospitality and remove the burden of my presence from you."

There was relief and satisfaction in Xer's expression as he rose to his feet. "Come, we will go to my brother Ptar's tent. The *nampu* [elders, seers, adults too old to fight, recordkeepers] are gathered there, too."

Max had not met Zel Ptar previously. He had been seriously wounded in whatever disaster had overtaken the Vinci and had needed time to recover. Even now he was plainly not well. He was propped in one of the portable beds the Enthok used, his skin a dull gray rather than its normal shining silver. Ptar was also a good deal older than Xers, his hair almost as dark as that of the nampu who sat on cushions around the tent.

"Pev Max," Ptar said formally, "be seated. How can I make you welcome?"

"I have eaten. I have drunk. I have slept," Max responded properly. "I have come to speak and to listen."

That ended the formalities. Ptar smiled. "We have most serious matters to discuss, but I have heard that about you which I cannot understand. Did you really make senseless, without injuring, three pevi?"

"Only two," Max laughed. "The third I tangled in a bola." He used the foreign word because there was none for that weapon in the language he now spoke. "That was pure luck, too. I am no expert in the use of the bola, but it is a marvelous hunting weapon, and I have been practicing with it."

"So the briski tell me. They are all afire to learn also."

"But none came to me to ask," Max said, and then slowly, "Do the briski fear my strange looks?"

"No," Ptar answered. "To ask for another's weapon or secret is forbidden among us—not so for you?" But then, before Max could reply to that, he added diffidently, as if he might be touching on a delicate subject, "The briski think you are a Bolvan—a people from the far north who are brown and have such eyes as yours. They do not notice that which no Bolvan, no Enthok, no other pev has."

An occasional pair of eyes glanced at his ears, at his five toes, and slid away.

"I am Quelv," an old female croaked. She was the oldest person there, shriveled and bent, her eyes and hair pitch black, her lips and tongue lighter than her dead gray skin. Max turned to her and nearly froze with surprise. She, and every other nampu, was equipped with a writing instrument and was busily scribbling away on a scroll of parchment. Nomads keeping written records? It was . . . odd—out of context. Max pushed the puzzle away when Quelve continued, "Are you from another world?"

Shock added to shock. Primitive people did not usually believe in life on other worlds, any more than primitive people kept records. And if they were not primitive . . .

"Yes," Max replied simply, "but I am pev. I am no Yelth or Trolg."

"It is written in the scrolls," Quelv muttered, "that the Old Ones moved from world to world. How did you come here?"

"I do not know," Max said. "I was sent out of my own world in a torment of pain and I woke here, alone and naked, two days' and one night's walking time, going from the direction of the sun's rising toward the sun's setting."

There was an uneasy stirring among the nampu, and the faintest shadow of a cold fear in Ptar's voice. "We do not know these lands well, but well enough to know that they are barren. You were hungry but not starving and you were not thirsty at all when you came to us. What did you eat and drink in those days of walking?"

"The water weed," Max replied, surpised at what was disturbing them.

Xers shook his head, his face creased with trouble. "No creature on this earth, save the Old Ones of the past, ever ate or drank from the water weed. Wet or dry, a little brings a deep sleep. A little more and you sleep forever."

"But I have said I am not of this earth, and that is easy enough of proof," Max exclaimed, thanking Yelth and Trolg and any other gods around that he had told the truth. "You see my body is different. Then inside my body there must also be differences—not many perhaps, because I can eat your food and drink your drink, but enough so that the water weed does not harm me. Let someone fetch sufficient weed and I will eat and drink of it here so that you may see."

Ptar stirred on his pillows and winced. Max was distressed to see that his explanations seemed to have made matters worse, for the Zel's expression was incredible—terrified and eager at the same time.

"That we will do." Ptar's voice was strained. "Not that we disbelieve you. Only a fool would lie about something so easy of proof. But I want to see it. It is not often a legend comes to life and walks among us."

"Hold on," Max protested. "I am no legend. Among my own people I was not of great importance. I was a teacher of battle arts—a good and respected teacher—but not more than that. I am not of the Old Ones of your legends. I have not their arts. I cannot go from world to world. To this world I was sent, and here I must stay until I die."

"Not an Old One?" Quelv's voice trembled with mingled relief and disappointment.

Max shook his head in determined negation. "I am an Earthman," using the Universum word although he knew they would not understand it. My people have traveled in space—once, a long, long time ago—but they never lived upon any other planet."

"Perhaps it is as well," Quelv remarked dryly. "From the legends we have, the Old Ones were prone to much trouble, and their ruined cities, most of them, did not die a peaceful death."

All eyes now fixed on Max unashamedly. There was a rising tension, but of eagerness, not fear. "Why were you sent?" Ptar asked.

It was as if the question had suddenly aroused a dormant but exquisite agony and simultaneously awakened a hope that a cure for that anguish might be found. Max closed his eyes, trying desperately to force his dream-revealed knowledge into his consciousness. Nothing came. He could tell them he had been banished for wrongdoing, but that would be a lie, he knew, as misleading as any other lie. This was too important to chance any lie or guess. Max opened his eyes and the distress in them met the hope and the pain in the eyes of the Enthok.

"I do not know," Max groaned. "I do not know." Hope leaped up in the silver eyes fixed on him. "Oh, no!" he cried. 'I beg you, do not believe I was sent in answer to your prayers. I do not mean I will not share your trouble, whatever it is. I will be glad to help in any way I can. But I am an ordinary pev, not a god or a legend sent to cure your hurt."

Ptar smiled. "Do not be so quick to take up so heavy a burden. Listen first to the tale of our woes. Then, if you still wish to cast in your lot with ours, forgive us if we hope a little. It is not every day that plain pev comes as you did to our world. Having come, why did you not walk *toward* the rising sun? And, had you not been clicking those rocks together just then, Xers would not have found you. You see?"

"I was clicking rocks for many bell-tenths, not just then," Max said mischievously.

He was not really trying to fight their conviction that "luck" or "fate" had sent him. Actually, he was wondering now whether there was something in the idea. Not luck or fate, perhaps, but it was not impossible that he had been set down at that time and place deliberately. It had occurred to him that even if Xers had not found him, he would soon have come to this camp. When he climbed the hill, he would have seen signs of the river, and then . . .

"Why were you clicking the rocks?" Xers interrupted his thoughts. "Did you not hope someone would hear?"

Max's explanation brought protests that fire could not be made from rocks on Gorona. Max's laughing assurances that it could brought forth the information that fire always came from the fire pits of the Old Ones and that those who went for it died horribly.

"They will die no longer," Max exclaimed. The fire pits of the Old Ones sounded revoltingly like some radioactive remains. He fetched his fire stones, gathered dried leaves crumpled into small pieces and very fine dry grass. When he struck the rocks together, a shower of sparks flew. The many voices gasped as one. The tinder had not caught, however. He struck again and again, close to the tinder—blew—a tiny thread of smoke curled upward. He blew again, most gently, fed more strands of grass, blew, another leaf—a tiny flame licked upward.

Quelv tottered forward, her hands outstretched. "Please," she quavered, "may I—"

Max put the stones into her hands. "They are nothing precious. Hard steel will work even better with some rocks. Set the briski to banging stones together by the river or to striking them with a knife blade and soon you will have sufficient store."

"And you say you are not our luck?" Xers remarked emphatically. "You have given us a gift of many lives."

"And he has more than paid his debt for fire, shelter, and food," Ptar interrupted. "So be warned. Though Max may be our luck, we may be his bane."

Silence descended again. Ptar had torn away the superficial covering of joy that the firestones had brought to expose again the deep unhealed wound.

"You cannot be my bane," Max said firmly. "We are quit of favor and obligation by my gift of the knowledge of the firestones. Thus, if I cast my lot with yours, I do it free of debt and of my own desire. Thus, only I may be my own bane. Now let me hear of this trouble."

Ptar shifted slightly again on his pillows. It seemed to Max that his skin was an even deader gray. He started to speak, then drew a weary breath. "Xers—"

"I will tell him, Ptar. Pev Max, from before we Enthok wrote our own scrolls, we have been hunters and fighters. We have never tilled fields nor herded flocks. When we found that skins and meat would not bring sufficient money to buy the goods we wanted, we offered our services as mercenaries. As this custom grew more fixed, the Bralidom [city dwellers] gave less and less thought to feats of arms. Because the Enthok will not leave their clans, they hired Bolvi to be Peacekeepers. Most Bralidom do not even own a sword, much less know what to do with one."

"Evil has come of the inability of the Bralidom to defend themselves," Ptar put in. "They have grown fearful and suspicious. For some years they have not trusted in the honor of the Enthok. They feared that—the battle won or lost—the Enthok would seize their city. Do not ask me for what purpose we would desire such a foul prize, but I suppose they value the place. They demanded hostages to ensure our honor."

"It is my fault!" Xers burst out, his mouth twisted, his eyes filling with tears. "I had heard what Sinkek of Salf was. It is my fault!"

"Xers! You spoke of what you heard."

"But I cast doubt upon what the Bolvan said—I laughed and said it was nothing to us that Sinkek was an evil pev."

"Nonetheless," Dragu, another of the nampu, comforted, "you spoke and we thought upon it."

"And Jael herself weighed the danger," Ptar said flatly.

Silence fell again, as if the name Jael had twisted a knife in a wound. Then Jael was the absent spirit here. Dead? Max did not think so. What he saw in the faces around him was not grief but an agony of fear and longing. Jael—the name drew him and also teased him with a sense of familiarity.

"Who is Jael?" Max asked.

"Our Thal." But Quelv saw the word was unfamiliar to Max. "She who is the mother of the future

Thal and Zeli. The heartbeat of our people. Our Royal Sister."

Xers had dropped his head into his hands. Ptar opened his eyes again. "Because Enthok fought Enthok for reasons that were none of their own, customs of mercy came naturally." His voice was weak and tears moved slowly down his cheeks, tracing a glittering line on the dull flesh. "The wounded were permitted to withdraw from battle and, although pevi died, it was seldom that death was desired for an opponent. Also it grew to a custom that any battle not decided on one day was followed by a three-day truce. The time was not long enough to bring more pevi or heal the wounded, so that any small advantage gained was maintained or even magnified, and the next battle brought a settlement."

"That was not sufficient for Sinkek." Xers took up the tale again. "We fought for Salf against the Enthok hired by the city of Degat, having left our Thal as hostage as was the custom." For an instant the trouble lifted from Xers's face and his eyes lit with enthusiasm. "It was a good fight. They were brave pevi and honest, and we fought with pleasure on both sides until the light failed. We drew apart at last because we could not tell foe from friend."

Max nodded, understanding. He had known such fights when he and another Master had grappled and kicked and struck long past the limits of endurance because of the pure joy of combat.

"So then the words of truce were cried upon both sides. They for Degat withdrew some two bibari to their camp and we, supporting and comforting our wounded, rode to the city." Xers's voice cut off suddenly, and his hands worked with hate, his skin darkening almost to black with passion.

41

"There were no supplies." In Ptar's voice there was also hate, but under it was a note of bewilderment, as if he could not believe it, even though he had lived through it.

"And he held your Thal hostage so you could not storm the city for your needs." Max heard his own voice grate with anger.

Unable to sit still, Xers rose and paced the tent, clenching and unclenching his hands and biting his lips with impotent rage. "Sinkek came to the wall and called out, demanding that we return to the battlefield and fall upon those who fought for Degat in the dark while they were eating and tending their wounded, without warning."

"I thought he jested," Ptar said. "I laughed."

"If Ptar was unwise in his laughter," Xers broke in, "I was foolish beyond measure in my rage. I spoke my mind, saying what would befall Sinkek. Then that urgel took thought to reality rather than his desire. First he proved that Jael was alive and unhurt—"

"And then," Max prompted because Xers's voice had failed again.

"So then I swallowed my gall," Ptar went on, "and I said we would not do what he asked, but if he held Jael unharmed we would defend Salf to the last drop of our blood."

"So you were defeated. That happens to every fighting clan." Max could see no reason to make his new friends relive their disaster in detail.

Xers nodded agreement to that. "The defeat would have been nothing, but there was no rest for us, no food, no balm for our wounds. Worse, for though spirit can uphold weak flesh, there were no forges for our smiths to mend our arms, no rods or feathers to fletch new arrows. We were overweary and under-armed. We fought neither wisely nor well. Blows that should have been caught and turned aside brought death. Weapons failed—"

He glanced at Ptar, whose face was wet with tears again. His brother ruler's weapon had failed, and his mate had missed a parry and was dead.

"At last," Xers hurried on, "even though we were fewer, the Enthok for Degat called the end of battle and quit the field. So much had we done, but we could do no more. We fled away in the night, fearing that Sinkek would set his Bolvi upon our nampu and briski."

Ptar drew a deep breath and wiped his face. "Now we wait for our wounds to heal that we may return and storm the city. We must trust to reach Jael before Sinkek can do her harm. We believe he will keep Jael with him to use as a shield for his own life. If Trolg and Yelth have not decided to wipe our clan from the tribe of Enthok—"

"No!" Max stated loudly and firmly. Every eye fixed on him with shock and horror. "Please forgive me," Max added hastily. "This is no way to speak where I am simply a guest, but what you are planning is madness."

Now some eyes shifted, and Xers's were veiled as he said, "You think it is too high a price to pay for one life?"

"No. Only the customs of your people and your own hearts can name the price of a single life among you, and the life of a hostage is worth more for honor's sake. But you will throw away that life as well as your own by this plan. There is an ancient writing of my people that says, 'To every thing there is a season,

43

and a time to every purpose under the heaven. A time to be born, and a time to die; . . . A time to kill, and a time to heal; . . . A time to weep, and a time to laugh.' There is also a time for force and a time for stealth. Is there not a single pev among you who will go with a new name to Salf and seek to find and free your Thal?"

"Is there one among us who would not go?" Xers burst out. "You know that path is closed to us!"

Obviously, there was something Max had missed. "Remember I am a stranger here. How is this path closed?"

"Do you think Sinkek has forgotten to tell his Bolvi that no Enthok may pass his gates?"

"But how—" Max began, and then smote his forehead with the heel of his hand. "How stupid I am. You Enthok are different in appearance from the Bralidom as the Bolvi are different from you."

"Yes, of course. Oh, we agree that this is a time for stealth—but there is no way to be stealthy." Xers made an exasperated gesture and Ptar added quietly, "We have thought of and even tried staining our skin and hair, but there is no way to hide our mouths and eyes."

"What is the appearance of the Bralidom?"

"They are green—of varying shades—with yellow eyes and their skin is smooth, like yours. The mouth is like rust, sometimes more orange, sometimes more dark red."

"I can see," Max said grimly, "that no art could change Enthok to Bralidom."

"Then you agree there is no way but to force the city. Will you come with us, Pev Max?" Xers asked eagerly.

"Certainly not!" Max exclaimed. And before the shock and pain of trust rejected could develop, he grinned broadly. "I can pass as a Bolvan. I will go to bring out the Thal by stealth."

Chapter 4

A stunned, unbelieving silence gripped the tent. Max looked from face to face, where incomprehension was giving way to hope, then to joy, and, finally, the blaze of joy was damped down by pangs of conscience. Max braced himself for argument. Honor was a good and necessary thing, but it sometimes made honorable beings hard to convince that a burden should be placed upon more appropriate shoulders. The protests were cut short by Quelv.

"Enough," she said. Her eyes passed around the semicircle of nampu and, one after another, they lifted their eyes from their writing and nodded. "Pev Max has offered and we believe that offer is made freely and truly of his own desire, also that he knows the danger into which he thrusts himself. Therefore it is time to accept with thanks or to tell him why he is unfit to undertake the task. This is the advice of the nampu to the Zeli."

A long discussion of pros and cons of a practical nature followed. Fortunately, language would not be a problem because Enthok was the lingua franca of the planet. If Max claimed to be from some distant area, no one would be surprised if his local language was incomprehensible.

"From where?" Max asked, wanting specifics.

"From far, far south, beyond the Helth Larth Jiz," Quelv said.

"Those are the ruined lands," Dragu protested. "How did he come alive through them?"

Another nampu grinned. "Who knows? Not he! The mind of a pev will not contain such horrors; it casts them out leaving a blankness behind. But to say he is from beyond the dead lands is good reason for having those things on his head and extra toes. It is known that some briski born after incautious travel in the ruined lands do not live and others are—different."

Ptar nodded gravely. "That will explain most differences in speech and appearance and even differences in custom. I say we should accept the offer of Pev Max." And the others readily agreed.

During the next week, weapons were readied, Max was drilled in the geography of the area, in as much of the Bolvan language as the clan knew, and taught the care and management of larths. What loomed largest in the discussions, however, was where, if Max was successful in arranging Jael's escape, they would meet the clan. The Vinci could not remain where they were because the game was diminishing. Moreover, because each city was in constant conflict and constantly shifting alliances with the others, Max and Jael could not expect asylum anywhere.

"But I do not understand," Max remarked. "If the Bralidom do not use arms, who will pursue us?"

"The Bolvi who have taken service with Salf. They are too wild a folk to fight together in groups, but they can fight and they are hunters and trackers of great excellence," Ptar answered.

"And it seems to me," Xers interrupted thoughtfully, "that there were many Bolvi in Salf, many, many more than would be needed for peacekeeping."

"Perhaps Sinkek looks to break custom in more ways than one," Max suggested. "If you broke open Degat, refusing to honor the truce as he first demanded, what would have happened?"

"I do not know," Ptar replied. "There is no custom for such a thing."

"Could Sinkek have sent his Bolvi into Degat and ruled both cities?"

There was a short silence. Then Ptar said slowly and distastefully. "I suppose he could. I do not know how the Bralidom of Degat regard their Zel. However, even if they loved him, what could they do? They are not armed and skilled in war. If Sinkek had sufficient Bolvi to beat those of Degat—"

"And then, using the wealth of both cities, could Sinkek hire two or even three clans of Enthok and turn upon the city of Pova?"

Xers passed his hand over his face, rubbing his eyes as if to wipe out the picture that was forming behind them. Ptar had started to say, "I do not believe the Enthok—" but Xers interrupted him.

"It could be. It could! Ptar, you are a wise Zel, but what did I say first and what did you and Jael agree to when I recounted the Bolvan's tale? I said that it was no matter to the Enthok that Sinkek was an evil pev. He was Bralidom, and the Bralidom must mind their own affairs. Would not other clans of Enthok think the same

48

way? Perhaps it is time the Enthok took thought about what and for whom they fight."

"It is against custom for the Enthok to interfere in the affairs of other tribes," Ptar said slowly but firmly.

"There is no need to interfere," Max suggested. "But would it be against custom for one clan to tell the other clans of Enthok how Sinkek has broken custom and what may come of this? Sinkek will not live to break custom again. That is the clan's right of vengeance. And that example may curb the other Zeli of the Bralidom, but what has happened once may happen again. The clans should be warned to watch for such a pattern."

"It is already entered in the scrolls, but you are right. It must be specially marked. We need no more dead cities—" Ptar stopped speaking suddenly and a grim smile touched his lips. "The arbas," he said. "Xers, the arbas! Jael can find it easily, and neither Bolvi nor Bralidom will follow there. You know both fear the dead cities."

"Is it safe for us?" Xers asked.

"We can camp south on the river and keep watch. The water flows north, so it is clean. Clans have done so many times. You know what is written. Only those who go to the fire pits sicken and die. Even those who ride with them and remain outside live."

"Some sickened later." Xers was still hesitant.

"Yes, but they lived. And they were close to the new fire coals. Jael knows the place of the fire pits. She can guide Max to a safe distance."

"Where and what is this arbas?" Max asked. The word meant dead-alive. Zombie or ghost was probably a good translation.

"It is a city of the Old Ones, lying on the southernmost tip of the sea. The Bralidom fear all the arbas to

49

madness. I said before that the Bolvi fear them, but I think it more likely that they would not go there for any purpose but their own."

"I agree," Xers said, laughing. "I do not believe the Bolvi fear anything. Those who survive their own fathers are not overgiven to fears."

"But it is still the best place to meet," Ptar insisted. Why, if a ship could be found, they could even come by sea from Salf."

Xers shuddered. Most Enthok hated sailing, but Max was interested and after some further discussion and explanation he agreed that the arbas sounded best. Then he yawned irresistibly. It was late and he had been crammed full of information. Xers and Ptar laughed and sent him off to bed saying, with some truth, that what he needed most urgently was time to digest the information he had rather than be given more information.

Outside the tent, Max glanced around and cursed vilely. He was completely disoriented again. By tradition the Enthok disturbed their surroundings as little as possible. They cut no green wood if dead was to be found. They hunted just enough to feed themselves and keep a supply of salted meat in reserve; not one animal more was taken and every bit of every animal was used. They even moved their tents—structures of such marvelous simplicity and efficiency that they virtually screamed aloud that a technological society had designed them—every day or two so that the grass would not suffer. And they could explain the ecological reasons for their actions. They had been taught and taught well. There was even a pattern to the movement which every small briski understood quite well—only Max could not fathom it. He was forever getting lost and having to be led to his destination.

The only tent he could invariably find was his own. That had been set up alone in a separate grassy hollow. At first Max had thought it was to keep him apart from the clan. Later he learned it was a courtesy to a stranger not to surround him with others so that he would feel free to come and go as he pleased. The tent had been moved several times, but always within the little hollow, and it was always quite alone.

What Max did not realize was that after his intention of rescuing Jael had been announced he was no longer considered a stranger. Thus, when he finally found his way through to his own little area, he walked into the first tent he came to—and walked in on Arile and Chelve making love in the lamplight.

They were very shocked and angry at first—lovemaking was a private matter among the Enthok—but realized almost immediately, from Max's strangled gasp of apology and stumbling exit, what had happened. They then pursued him, as soon as their kilts were in place, led him to his own tent, and said they were sorry they had not told him of their intention of moving their tent into his area.

With sparkling eyes and giggles, Arile said, "Eh, then, Pev Max, you have seen—all too clearly—how it is done here on Gorona. Is it different upon your world?"

Chelve kicked her gently, but she pushed him away and insisted, "But I want to know!"

Max felt as if anyone could light a candle at his ears. "No," he replied as steadily as possible, "it is not different. On my world it is the same."

"Oh, Pev Max," Arile cried, "would you show me—"

At which point Chelve lost any desire for subtlety, clapped one hand over his mate's mouth, and dragged

51

her forcibly from Max's tent. Max listened for a moment anxiously, but as soon as he heard Arile giggling over Chelve's growls about bad manners, he was at least relieved of any fear that he had made trouble between the couple. He knew that the sexual customs of the Enthok encouraged promiscuity in youth but, while permitting divorce, required monogamous sexuality in marriage.

Whatever Arile wanted—embarrassment choked Max again and then was swallowed down in a wash of pleasure. Chelve's member had been almost identical with his own in size and shape in the brief but unforgettable glimpse he had had of it in passionate distension. Max had not previously had time to think about sex, but now a slow smile curved his lips. It was very nice to know there was no need for him to remain celibate for the rest of his life. He was suddenly quite anxious to start for the city. However different their race, the emotional quality of the people of Gorona was very similar to *Homo sapiens'*. Thus, where there was the complexity of city life, there would be males and females plying the oldest profession.

"Naughty, naughty," Max reproved himself. "Business first, then pleasure."

A week later, in midafternoon, Max topped a low rise and looked down at Salf to gasp in surprise. The Enthok were a highly civilized people with respect to literature, art, and music, but they knew nothing of physical luxury and they had not the slightest interest in cities. When Max had asked, they could say only that the Zel's stronghold was on the northeast side and seemed to be separated from the main city wall by a large garden.

The talk of walls and strongholds had led Max to expect a town resembling descriptions of medieval cities that he had read. But here, instead of a raw, brutal stronghold of crude stone surrounded by mud, wattle, and half timbered hut houses, was Byzantium in all its glory. Max pulled Beulah (the larth) to a halt and gaped quite openly. The walls were there and they surrounded the city completely—at least as much of it as Max could see—but the stone was cut and polished and the great gates that faced the road carried scrolls, flutings, and panels worked exquisitely in polished bronze. Above the walls and gates, a forest of cupolas lifted, dressed in more brilliant hues than Max could name. To the right, all gilded and glittering under the lavender sky, rose the mightiest towers of all. Stronghold? Nonsense! Sinkek must live in a palace.

A few bell-tenths later, Max was enlisted in the Peacekeeping force of Salf. He was a little surprised at how easy it was, but apparently Sinkek was paying far above the usual rate to his Bolvi and word of his generosity had spread widely. Max had discovered that the visual delights glimpsed from the hill above the city were not so apparent on closer examination. Behind the great gates he had seen unsavory gaggles of hovels and delapidated buildings. The olfactory impact of Salf was also less than thrilling. Frankly, the city stank. He began to think the Enthok had considerable reason for avoiding cities.

Max had also discovered that his worst fears were facts. Sinkek was training the undisciplined Bolvi into an effective commando force. He had made a bad mistake with the Enthok, but he had learned his lesson. Perhaps he was still hoping to find a clan with weaker principles than Clan Vinci, but he was also preparing to invade Degat, or some other city, by stealth. The citizens' lack of ability to defend themselves brought such an ambition easily within the realms of possibility because, according to Xers, the number of Bolvi Peacekeepers in a city was usually small.

Moreover, the Bolvi were an ideal tool for Sinkek's purpose. They had no feeling of kinship for the Bralidom, and they had very little more for each other. The young were only interested in gaining strength and battle skills so that they could eventually go back to their homeland and gather a pride of females. The wages they earned, those that they did not spend on weapons and free females, were invested in fine cloth and other goods with which to tempt females to join them. The older males, who had given up hope of this form of heaven, had usually taken a Bralidom female. In any case, by tradition and perhaps even a genetic trait, no Bolvan male would think twice before he assaulted or killed another Bolvan male.

It was against custom! Max was surprised by his surge of anger and at the same time he was wryly amused because he was slipping into expressing his feelings in Gorona terms. Nonetheless, he had not bothered to read the service agreement he signed. If he had been signing away his soul or agreeing to commit five murders a week, he would have signed. The only way into Salf was through the Peacekeepers, and the only way to stop Sinkek was to rescue Jael and find a way for the Vinci to enter the city.

Chapter 5

Max's enlistment among the Bolvi Peacekeepers worked out as he had hoped. The first week was devoted to testing his skills and patience and permitting him to become acquainted with the external environs of the palace. Max's only difficulty was in concealing his abilities at unarmed combat. He was only a moderate swordsman, a trifle better than average for a Bolvan but not remarkably so. At the end of this period, the Manili was assured that Max was competent with weapons and not prone to fly into a rage when he was given an order or without strong provocation.

There was no training in drilling or maneuvering. Bolvi were useless for organized battle, although they made superb commandos. Obviously the next step was on-the-job training, and Max was delighted to hear that he would be detailed for duty inside the palace until he knew enough about the Bralidom nobility not to step on any toes inadvertently when he was on duty in the city.

Nothing could have been better. He was assigned to an experienced guard to learn the geography of the palace, which was complex, and the behavior expected when dealing with the nobility. The best part of it all was that, for once, any questions Max asked would seem normal. Max's only concern was that Kole would be so annoyed at being constantly in the company of another male that he would be a surly and unwilling teacher.

This, however, was not the case. Kole had come young to Salf and had found Bralidom females and Bralidom luxury more to his taste than his own customs. He had even taken on many of the Bralidom ways and was willing enough to instruct Max. In fact, when he realized that Max was friendlier than the usual young Bolvan, Kole was even willing to gossip.

"There are as many levels up as down, and we do not go on duty until evening bell. Shall we begin with the lords or the slaves?"

"The slaves," Max replied.

He found it an effort to sound indifferent. This was something he knew he must face sooner or later in a relatively young society. He had read enough history to be aware that prisons and torture chambers abound all through the developmental period of any social system. Then the system either breaks down completely or outgrows the need for such methods. Certainly Hax had no intention of reforming the penal system on Gorona. It was not his purpose—and if it had been he would have fought the compulsion. The time was not ripe for that, nor would it be ripe for many generations after Max was dead. All that troubled him was whether he would be able to behave as expected.

It was even possible that Jael would be among the prisoners. Max did not think that was really likely— she was too important to be thrust into a dungeon— but it was necessary to eliminate even the remote possibility. In any case he wished to get the bad part over with. As illogical and amoral as it was, Max felt sure his tour of the Byzantine splendor of the nobles' quarters would blur the image of the suffering below. And, because he was powerless to do anything about the suffering, it was senseless for him to carry the burden of it.

Kole and Max walked along behind the screening grove which curved gently toward the mass of interconnected towers and lower buildings that made up the palace. Well to the rear, a single guard lounged beside a low door. He hardly glanced at the pass Kole bore—a pass Max had examined very carefully indeed —and waved them through. A short corridor, flagstoned and ill lit, opened out into an equally ill-lit antechamber, which contained a large double door opposite the corridor and a smaller door closed with a heavy bar to the left.

Another guard cursorily examined their pass, then unbarred the small door. A second guard stood at ease before the double doors which, as Max suspected, led to the formal reception chambers of the palace. They went through the small door, Kole warning Max that the stairs began directly. There were three levels, and they went all the way down, Max concentrating on controlling both his expression and his tendency to shudder as the light grew even dimmer and the air grew danker and thicker. At the lowest level, Kole pounded on the door. A coarse voice croaked what was obviously an obscenity in a language Max could not understand. Kole replied viciously in Enthok, and

57

heavy steps slogged across the floor. A key grated in a stiff lock. The door swung heavily open. Max could not restrain a hiss of surprise. Facing him was the fattest pev he had ever seen.

"Well?" she croaked in Enthok.

Kole held up his pass. "Pev Max is to be shown the prisons."

A laugh like a gargle preparatory to spitting came out of her, and her dirty brown-green hide looked to be in danger of splitting as the flesh inside it shook. "A warning to behave himself?" She turned away without waiting for an answer, relocked the door, took a torch from a holder beside it. "Come then."

Another door on the other side of the room, which was furnished with a heavy rough-hewn table and benches, although closed tight was unlocked. Max could feel his heart beating in his throat. Ahead, when the warder opened the door, was a blackness almost as absolute as that in the Transporter. The torch cast a flickering light a bar or two ahead of their guide and then was swallowed up.

A low whimper brought another hiss from Max and another gargling chuckle from the jailor. "After a while," she wheezed, "the light hurts their eyes."

A short silence followed during which they came abreast of a cell that was little more than a niche hewn into the stone. Max was almost afraid to look. If Jael had uttered that whimper, she had been damaged more mentally or physically than her kinsmen suspected. However, it was a very youthful Bralidom male that clung to the front bars. When he saw the two Bolvi, he almost cowered back, but he checked the fearful gesture and drew himself up straighter. Max was moved by an immediate liking for so young a pev who, helpless as he was, fought off fear. He was also impressed by the courage with which the young pev looked into the light, although the pain it caused him was obvious.

"Rest easy," the jailor remarked, "they have not come for you."

That too was a revelation. The tone was flat and indifferent. If the jailor had no sympathy for the poor imprisoned creature, neither did she take pleasure in his fear.

"Leave the light," the prisoner gasped. "Please leave the light. I am going mad."

"Torches cost money," the jailor replied. "While you paid, you had light."

"But I have no more money. I will pay you double or triple when I am released. I will give you a better position. I will—"

"Drail Zabulin," the jailor cut him off sharply. "I do my duty here according to custom and order. No special order has come about you from the Zel. Therefore, if you have money, or someone outside will send money, I will give you light. If not, you lie in the dark. Perhaps your brother the Zel desires that you be mad. Perhaps he merely wishes to lesson you. What the great ones do is nothing to me. I do my duty."

"Please—" the prisoner sobbed, but the jailor was already moving on.

Max ground his teeth silently to keep his mouth shut. There had been no need for that speech. The jailor had—within the strict bounds of her duty—taken the opportunity to give the prisoner a few seconds of light. But it would do no good for Max to offer to leave money and make himself an object of suspicion. Perhaps when Sinkek was removed all prisoners would be released. Besides, as appealing as the young creature was, perhaps his punishment was deserved.

They passed another niche cell on the other side. The prisoner in that one did not stir. Max permitted his breath to ease out slowly when the torchlight showed a scabrous green hide.

"He will die soon," the jailor remarked. "When they are in the dark too long, they die. This one does not eat anymore."

The flat statement contracted Max's stomach. Suddenly he thought of a safe question. "What is Drail?"

Kole looked at him in surprise and then nodded comprehension. The word was from the Bralidom language because neither the Bolvi dialects nor Enthok had any equivalent term. "Drail is the title for any member of the royal family."

"The royal family?" Max echoed. "Is that first prisoner a hostage then?"

The jailor's thick chuckle preceded her speech. "Is this the way to treat a royal hostage? No. This is the Zel's youngest brother, although his egg came from a lesser female. Nonetheless, he was a favorite and the old Zel named him Drail."

Max made himself shrug as if he had lost interest, but his mind was busy. Quite aside from sympathy, it was necessary to keep this young Drail sane if possible. If Zabulin was here, then he was either opposed to Sinkek originally or had good reason to hate him now. From the young pev's manner, his spirit was not yet broken. Max was still not familiar with the political setup in Salf, but Zabulin might be an important pawn.

A few steps further along the corridor, Max tripped, uttered a curse, and knelt to give a savage tug at his sandal thongs. Not surprisingly the overstrained leather snapped. With another imprecation, Max slipped off the now useless sandal, hobbled a few steps, and then took off the other. Kole asked him if he wanted to go back and get another pair, but Max laughed and replied that he would rather have cold, bruised feet than walk up and down all those stairs again. Next he hitched at his belt, in which he had stuck his sandals, as if to settle it more comfortably. Actually he moved it so that his pouch was on the far side of the torchlight. Then, silently, he gathered about half the coins in the pouch and, thanking Yelth and Trolg that the coins were square, began to wrap the sandal thongs around them.

One-handed, this was so complicated a task that he saw only enough of the four other prisoners confined along the passage to be sure they were Bralidom. He was grateful to his preoccupation, which also prevented him from taking in fully the attractions of the torture chamber. This was a huge vault which, from the sound of running water in the background, Max thought might be partly natural. The gross jailor was rather proud of the room itself and went about lighting torches to show its extent. She seemed, to do her justice, totally disinterested in the instruments—they were not her business; she was a jailor, not an executioner, but the cavern was a marvel.

Max's preoccupation was made easier by the fact that the chamber was not in use. It was also the last stop on the tour of the lowest level. After Max had exclaimed his appreciation of the huge vault, the torches were carefully extinguished and they retraced their steps. This time Max lagged a step or two behind, pretending to feel his footing with caution to spare his feet. Carefully he ran his fingers along the right-hand wall, counting silently. When he had counted three barred doors, he took the leather-bound parcel of coins from his pouch. At the fourth door, he cast it quickly between the bars.

Max could only hope that Zabulin would notice it in the faint glimmer of light that remained after the torch had passed his cell. He hoped too that the young Drail still retained sufficient self-control not to cry out at once for light. He had some hope of this because the prisoner did not, this time, either whimper or rush toward the light. Max was almost caught in the act. The thud the coins made in falling was very soft, but the jailor turned her head at once.

"What was that?" she muttered, casting a sudden suspicious glance at Kole and Max and turning back.

So Zabulin had friends, Max thought. Bolvi could not be suspected of passing a Bralidom anything for private reasons. That the jailor checked indicated that she might have been warned against such an attempt. Max flexed his knees and readied his hands, cursing at the too ready sympathy that had led him to make such a mistake. He could knock out Kole and the warden, but how to get out of here?

Just as the jailor reached Zabulin's cell, however, there was another dull thud. The tension eased out of her. "Stop that," she said sharply. "You will only damage yourself, and that is foolish."

The prisoner stared at her sullenly, but he dropped the fist with which he had struck the wall. Max's hopes soared. There was no sign of the thong-bound coins on the floor of the cell. If Zabulin could still think that quickly, there was an excellent chance that he would use Max's gift judiciously and that the very fact that he had received such a gift would help keep him stable. First, it would give him hope, remind him that he had friends; second, it would give him something to think about, wondering who this particular friend was.

Fortunately Kole showed no disposition to linger, nor, surprisingly, did the jailor seem to want them to stay. Soon they were knocking for admittance to the middle level. Here there were many more cells and they were all filled, some even containing more than one prisoner. There were other chambers, too, the jailor told them, stretching away under the other great halls, but they were all the same and not worth seeing. The warden, an ordinary-looking Bralidom male, with dull green-brown skin and exquisite green-laced golden eyes, was quite chatty, informing his guests without being asked of the various crimes the prisoners had committed. In many ways the conditions were worse than on the lower level. The crowding produced stench, and many prisoners showed injuries. Some were the results of a session in the torture chamber, where information about confederates and hidden loot was extracted, but most were inflicted by the prisoners on each other.

Max did not feel the sense of oppression he had experienced below, or the feeling of outrage. There was light; there were voices; and there was the sense that these men deserved their incarceration. The whole was no more than melancholy. The top level, by contrast, was almost cheerful. The section they inspected was made up of four large chambers facing a central area in which several jailors were occupied. One willingly abandoned his task and showed Kole and Max around. Each large cell was lit and ventilated by short shafts to the surface and was reserved for a related group of minor offenses. One was filled with debtors, another with drunks, a third with brawlers and other breakers of the peace, a fourth with swindlers, petty thieves, and other cheaters of various types.

If the air was not salubrious, it was breathable. The conditions were crowded, but most of the prisoners were talking to each other—probably, Max thought cynically, exchanging tricks of the trade so that the more innocent emerged with new and better ideas. What was most interesting, however, was that traffic was fairly heavy. While Max and Kole were there, a jailor began to call a list of names. The prisoners lined up at the cell gate, which was slid back to allow one to pass through at a time. Each prisoner gave his name, received a pass, and finally the group was shepherded out by another jailor.

Max's brain began to buzz. If Zabulin could be disguised and a pass obtained for him as, say, a drunkard, he could be got past the upstairs door. The Bolvi guard there would have no way of knowing which level he really came from. How to get him out of the first door, Max had as yet no idea, but it was at least a ray of hope for an escape. Provided, Max told himself sternly, that Zabulin's escape would serve any purpose. He must not permit his sympathy for the young Drail to obscure his main purpose or, worse, to endanger his chances of carrying out that purpose.

Chapter 6

Max had been raised in a technological society. It leaned toward smooth, highly polished surfaces that were easy to clean, to gentle curves that were soothing to the eye, and to pastel colors that calmed and relaxed the mind. Only in his reading, in illustrations, and in paintings and hangings faded and tattered by age, was he acquainted with magnificence for its own sake. The reality of it was stunning.

His first impression of the Great Halls, the formal reception chambers of the palace, was of the riot of color. Purple, red, malachite green, royal blue, crimson, orange, and yellow assaulted his senses so that his heartbeat quickened with excitement. Then he began to pick out patterns. But it was too much—of everything. Floors of dizzying mosiac, walls patterned and inlaid with sparkling minerals, pillars fluted and gilded, rising to vaulted and painted or gilded ceilings, gigantic paintings, murals, and tapestries all lighted by huge windows in deep embrasures roiled his brain and left him as open-mouthed with wonder as the most uncivilized barbarian. Kole was pleased and amused by his reaction.

"You have no great cities in your southern land," he said.

Max shook his head speechlessly and remained silent while they zigzagged through several other huge chambers differentiated from each other only by their decoration and interconnected in devious ways. When they finally returned to the first Hall, the only one Max could recognize, he finally spoke. "For the sakes of Yelth and Trolg, do not leave me. I would die of thirst and hunger before I found my way out."

Kole assured him that he would soon grow accustomed to the passages and, indeed, might never have an occasion to return to most of them except in company with other guards, but Max hardly heard him. His brain was buzzing again. Amidst his confusion one thing stood out clearly. There were no guards in the audience chambers.

"Does no one guard these precious things?" he asked at last.

"For what? There are guards at the entrances. Can you think of a way to hide and remove any of the furnishings or hangings? Or how long it would take to scrape off enough gilding to make a sum worth the effort? There are guards for show and to protect the Zel when he uses the chambers, of course. The things are safe."

There was the faintest emphasis on the word *things*, which led Max to believe that Kole was aware of the dissatisfaction with Sinkek and that the dissatisfaction was not confined to the rural or common people, who would have no business in the Great Halls. "Then what do we guard?" he asked suggestively.

"Come," Kole remarked with a wry grin. "I will show you."

He turned toward the apparently blank rear wall of the reception room they were in, passed behind a tapestry, which Max now saw did not hang flat against the wall, and opened a small door. Max hissed with surprise. "Do all the rooms have secret doors?"

"There is nothing secret about them. They lead always to the living chambers on the floor above. You would not have royalty running through public corridors and being bumped about by the common herd, would you?"

The note of sarcasm was even stronger this time, but Max chose to take what was said literally. "No. It would be dangerous. The higher the station the more the enemies," he added sententiously. And then, with a frown: "But it does not seem very safe to have these unguarded doors leading to the private parts of the palace either."

Kole shrugged. "If the Zeli had given themselves less to building more and more magnificent palaces, such doors might be guarded. There are so many doors and passages that it would take all the Bolvi alive to guard them. But it does not matter. You will see. Only a very small part of the second level is occupied, and that is well enough guarded."

Better and better, Max thought. "But then what is on the third level?"

"The palace servants are quartered there, and," he added with a sly grin, "the unofficial members of the royal family. The males and females the Zel keeps for his pleasure who belong officially to others. Some we guard. Some come and go as they please. And I suspect, though I am careful not to *know,* that there are parts of the third level that are occupied of which even the Zel is unaware." Kole looked over his shoulder at the empty room, giving the first sign of uneasiness he had shown. "There is even," he said in a lowered voice, "an Enthok female."

Jael! Max's heart leaped and checked. He knew she was still alive. Because he had no idea how an ordinary Bolvan would take such information, he looked as blank as possible and said, "What?"

Kole nodded portentously. "I tell you because you are an outlander and it may be your customs are different from ours. If her clan had not been all but wiped out, there would have been more work for us than I would like, though I complain often enough that there is too much game-playing and too little peace-keeping. Perhaps there would have been no Sinkek to pay your hire and no Salf to come to."

Max stared at Kole and said slowly, "And is it so sure they will not still return?"

"Your Enthok are the same as those here," Kole chuckled wryly. "Of course they will return, but it is believed there are so few remaining that they can accomplish little."

"And because it is so believed, none has been set to watch?" Max asked coldly with raised brows.

Kole chuckled again and lowered his voice still more. "Sinkek may be mad, but he is not stupid. A day after the battle we remained within the walls to be sure they were not merely regrouping. The next day the trackers went out. We dropped their trail in the mountains— they were far enough away to be no danger. Sinkek has sent messengers north and south to inquire, but none has seen the clan. Many could not so easily conceal themselves, so they are either very few or very far away. But a watch is still set and incomers are questioned."

"Ah, yes." Max nodded. "I remember. I wondered why the Manili was more interested in Enthok groups that showed signs of battle than anything else." Then he shook his head. "Still, I do not believe they will abandon their pev."

"Neither do others. Many have advised Sinkek to cast her out of the city now that her clan is gone, but the Zel thinks they will seek revenge for their hurts and holds her as hostage." Kole again cast uneasy glances over his shoulders and, almost whispering, added, "I think he has other reasons too. Bralidom males have mated with Enthok females before—"

"In Salf?" Max asked unbelievingly.

"Not in any city. Sometimes a young exile will join the Enthok—one who cares less for the ring of coins than the ring of swords. They will take anyone in. They are a friendly people, but—" Kole shook himself distastefully—"they live one on top of the other and change their females as I change my kilt."

To that Max made no objection. Certainly that was the way it would look to a Bolvan. He confined himself to the main theme of Kole's story. "But why? Are there not enough Bralidom females for him? Is the Enthok so beautiful?"

"Beautiful? Ay, even to a Bolvan, to whom that skin looks like a month-old corpse, and Sinkek is lecherous enough to be a Bolvan rather than a Bralidom." (Max knew that to be a compliment, not an indictment.) "But that, I think, is only a side purpose." Kole dropped his voice still lower so that Max had to lean toward him to hear. "Thus far Sinkek's young have not been—" The hardened soldier shuttered and swallowed hard. "Never mind. It is better not to speak

of that at all, nor even to think about it. But consider
a Zel with the devious mind of the Bralidom and the
courage and interest in war of the Enthok. It is whispered that Sinkek dreams of raising such a Drail—or
that he has been told to raise such a one."

Max just stared for a moment. "Who could tell a
Zel, and such a Zel as Sinkek—"

But Kole had gone further than he meant to, se-
duced by Max's eagerness to listen. His face froze. "No
one. Moreover, we have talked too much already of
matters that are no affair of ours. Let us go up."

Max repressed the sudden stirring of purpose inside
of him and followed Kole up the narrow stair. They
came out in a tiny entranceway again screened from
the main corridor by a tapestry. And when they had
pushed past into the wide corridor beyond, Max saw
that there was one other hanging a way down the opposite wall which must curtain another doorway. Here,
however, there were guards enough. To the right,
there were two ornate closed doors on the opposite
side of the corridor and one on the side where they
stood. To the left were two doors on their side and one
opposite. Before each door a Bolvan guard stood, relaxed but alert. Beyond, in both directions, were cross
corridors along which Max could not see.

"This is the occupied wing where you will stand
guard." Kole gestured toward the left cross corridor.
"Those are Zel Sinkek's quarters. We will not go there.
Come this way and I will show you where you will be
stationed tonight."

They turned right. The left arm of the corridor was
very short and a tall window looking out on the garden
filled most of the outer wall. There was no tapestry to
indicate a stairwell, but one guard who stared at them
with faint hostility stood at a closed door. Kole was

just about to turn right again into the longer arm of the corridor when the door opened suddenly and a small green hurricane burst out.

"Fool! Did you not hear me call to you to open the door?"

The guard jumped. "No, noble one. I am sorry. Those—"

"You—" she had begun when his gesture made her turn her head and she caught sight of Max and Kole. Kole started to back away into the corridor they had come from, but he was not quick enough. "Stop!" the imperious Drail cried. "Come here!"

As Kole and Max approached, Drail Delvinia pushed in front of the guard. Max, who could see her clearly for the first time, hissed aloud.

"What did you make that sound for?" she snapped furiously.

Max bowed deeply. "I beg your pardon, noble one. You are the most beautiful female I have ever seen in my whole life. Forgive me for my amazement."

If Max was laying on flattery with a trowel in an effort to pacify the petulant Drail, he was still not far off. His hiss had been caused by amazement at her beauty. All the Bralidom Max had seen until this moment were the lower-class farmers and servants. Their muddy green-brown skins and dull sandy hair made ordinary even the most regular and attractive features. Delvinia, however, was a horse—or, rather, a reptile—of another color entirely.

Her skin had the color, polish, and glitter of an emerald of the first water, out of which her golden eyes glowed like clear torches. Her hair was a cascade of dark gold over her back and shoulders. The nails of the hand she had raised to point were also gold. She wore the kilt that seemed a universal garb for all in

71

Gorona, but the kilt was of some diaphanous material of pale blue belted around her narrow waist by a thick girdle of worked gold studded with gems. Gold sandals shod her delicate feet.

The petulance in her face abated somewhat. "And who are you to call a Drail beautiful?"

"No one, noble one, which is why I asked pardon for my presumption. I am only a new Bolvan guard. Max is my name."

"Max? That is not a Bolvi name."

There was no safe riposte to that. Disagreement on even so minor a point could be dangerous. Max bowed deeply again. "I am from the far south, noble one, from beyond the ruined lands, and our tongue is different."

A gleam of interest replaced the petulance that seemed Delvinia's normal expression and made her even more attractive. "You came across the Deadlands? How?"

"Noble one, I am not sure myself. I remember little beyond hunger and thirst and—horror. I try not to think of it."

"I do not believe you! Do you know what it costs to lie to a Drail?"

Without another word, Max removed his helmet and turned his head a little. This time it was Delvinia that hissed. She came closer, eyes bright with excitement and put out a hand as if to touch Max's ear gently. Instead, quite suddenly, she pulled it sharply with all her strength. Unprepared, Max howled with pain and clapped a hand to his head. Delvinia trilled with laughter.

"They are real!" she exclaimed. "What did you say your name was?"

"Max," he replied softly, seething inwardly. He was

too well disciplined to give way to his initial rage, and, as the smart eased, he told himself that she might merely be spoiled.

Delvinia had turned her golden eyes to Kole. "And what are you doing here?"

"It was ordered that I show Pev Max the palace and the place where he is to stand guard so that he might not lose himself when it is his time for duty."

"And do you think you have learned your way around?" The laughter trilled again as she turned back to Max.

"No," he answered with obvious sincerity. "Indeed, I am sure I will *never* learn."

A peculiar smile lifted her beautiful lips. "Do you think you can find your way back here?"

Max was aware that the young guard had been following the conversation closely. Now he saw him stiffen and heard the faintest suggestion of a growl of smothered rage. It was unlikely that the Bolvi considered anyone they guarded as their property, so there must be some more personal relation between this particular guard and the Drail. That meant trouble if the question Delvinia asked Max was a hint of interest on her part. Nonetheless, Max saw more pros than cons to feeding that interest.

"If it is *your* order, noble one, I will find my way— whether I know it or not," he responded. There was, he hoped, just the right amount of suggestiveness in the remark without anything that could be obvious presumption.

"Then find your way here after the evening bell, Max, and we will see what other odd features you bring with you from south of the Deadlands."

"I have duty after evening bell, noble one, but I am

sure that if you order that duty to be changed—" Max left the words hanging and she took the bait.

"I do so order," she said haughtily to Kole. "You hear me."

"I hear you, Drail Delvinia. I will so report to the Manili."

The smothered growl came again, but Max did not permit his eyes to wander. He hoped Delvinia would deal with the other guard, but without much confidence. She was closer and must have heard the Bolvan's reaction. More likely she would enjoy knowing she had engendered enmity between the two males. It would tickle her fancy that they should fight over her, Max guessed. Then he wondered whether he could stave off a showdown until he found Jael.

Delvinia, having issued her order, simply walked past them as if they no longer existed. The guard followed, casting a single glance at Max that boded no good. Kole formed his mouth to hiss, but did not permit any sound to pass his lips. He waited until Delvinia had disappeared around the corner of the corridor and then led Max back in the direction they had come.

Chapter 7

In the soft light of the scented oil lamps, Max looked again at the strewn table, fixing in mind the position of the small seal he had seen Delvinia using. It was at least something to do while he was being examined as if he were a stud stallion. Max found the sensation of being so minutely examined peculiar. He was not particularly modest, and his culture had no prohibition against nudity, but he could not understand why his genitals merited such very particular attention. What was more, the fact that it was Delvinia that was conducting the examination made him nervous.

Less and less did Max like the expression in her exquisite golden eyes with their lacework of brilliant green. Long golden talons scratched gently, oh so gently. Max had a double reaction that knotted the muscles in his abdomen and quickened his breathing. Delvinia giggled.

"Are you afraid of me, Max?"

"Yes, noble one," he replied, just a trifle breathlessly.

To tell the truth, he was and he was not. He was not afraid she could hurt him again. Forewarned now, Max could render Delvinia unconscious before her hand could close. But such a move would sorely interfere with the accomplishment of his purpose.

"That is very wise. I am a dangerous Drail," she murmured. She touched him again, gently, skillfully. Max's reaction intensified. "And do you feel nothing but fear?" Her murmur was even more dulcet, inviting.

"You can see for yourself that I desire you," Max replied. He was trembling slightly and his voice was not completely steady.

"And which do you feel most strongly."

Max choked back a chuckle. She could laugh at him, but he was sure she was not the type that could endure being laughed at in return. "Desire."

"That too is wise."

Delvinia had been kneeling in front of Max, the better to see and feel, but now she rose and held out her arms in unmistakable invitation. Max stepped forward without hesitation. It had been a long time, and she was very beautiful. And, no matter how dangerous it was to accept Delvinia's invitation, Max was sure it would be far more dangerous to reject her. Now he acted exactly as he would have done with a woman of his own world, except for indulging in somewhat more extended foreplay.

At first Delvinia had seemed surprised. It was obvious that she was accustomed to being the aggressor in love, but she liked Max's innovation well enough to respond with quite marked enthusiasm. Best of all,

Max noticed that the peculiar look in her eyes had melted into a far more normal expression of simple lust. All in all it was a most satisfactory interlude for both of them. Finally Max eased himself away from the gasping Drail and smiled at her. Her luminous eyes were still dazed, their green lacework dimmed and blurred by exhaustion.

"Did I please you, noble one?" he murmured.

"You surprised me," she sighed. "You certainly surprised me. You are like no lover I have ever had before."

"Your surprise was pleasant, I hope?"

That drew laughter from her. "Oh, you Bolvi. You must always be patted and flattered by a female. Yes, then, pleasant." She raised herself upon an elbow and stared at Max's naked body, then shook her head. "But why do your members not sink back into your body as those of the northern males. When I first looked at you I thought you were lustful already, but now—"

For one moment Max was shocked speechless. Because of the friction between Bolvi males, each guard had his own tiny room. With the Enthok also, Max had had private quarters. Thus, he had never (except for that brief glimpse of Chelve) seen a naked Goronian. He had not realized until this moment that their sexual organs, like those of any lizard, were normally retracted into the body. No wonder Delvinia had been fascinated by him.

"We who cannot retract our organs are always fertile," he blurted, aware that he had been silent too long.

Delvinia gasped and jerked completely upright, her eyes blazing. "You mean that you may have bred to an egg of mine?" she hissed.

77

Max knew that was totally impossible, but before he could think of a way to explain without betraying his offworld origin, Delvinia began to laugh.

"It is nothing. I can break the egg. But how funny. Sinkek seeks an Enthok half blood because—" The laughter checked. The eyes the Drail turned on Max were now completely mad. "Perhaps Bithe is right," she whispered. "Perhaps a half blood would not be—" The green-webbed eyes stared at Max until he was afraid he would begin to sweat. "I hope," Delvinia murmured dulcetly, "that those things on your head do not make you hear better than other pevi."

"I have been both blind and deaf since I entered these apartments," Max assured her fervently.

She stared at him speculatively for a moment more, then nodded. "It had better be so," she remarked with a vicious smile. "To touch a Drail as you have touched me is an offense for which the punishment is the death of a thousand days. So long as you are silent—and useful—you will live. You will stand this watch every night. Fail once, and I will accuse you. Try to escape and I will have the hunters out after you. Get to your post."

Gratefully, Max slid out of the bed, snatched his kilt, his sandals, and one seal from the desk in the outer chamber, and eased himself out of the door as silently as possible. He leaned against the wall in the corridor after dressing and hurriedly disposed of the stolen trinket in the coil of hair under his helmet. Events were really getting out of hand. No gambling tout in his right mind would give any odds at all on how long Delvinia's present mood would last. And whether her next mood would be to order Max killed or to try again for a half-blooded briska was equally incalculable.

No wonder Delvinia's other pet guard had growled. Not only was his genetic tendency to maintain a pride assaulted, but if he were supplanted his life might be in danger. Doubtless he believed that safety for him lay in eliminating Max as soon as possible, before Delvinia came to a definite decision about which male she preferred. Max knew that, unlike Bolvi females, Delvinia could not be coerced by his death, but he also knew he would never be able to convince the Bolvan of that.

A huge yawn forced its way out of him. Max pushed himself free of the wall and began to pace silently back and forth in front of the door. All he needed was to be caught asleep at his post and have the Manili out for his blood too. He had to find Jael and he had to find her soon. If the Bolvan guard didn't get him, Delvinia would. And even if he managed to keep both of them at bay, he would not be able innocently to claim he was lost after a day or two more.

The remainder of that tour of duty Max acted as if he were on the verge of falling flat on his face. When the Manili's deputy checked on him, he was pacing groggily, and when Delvinia's servants peered out at him from time to time, he did not try to conceal the yawns that were racking him even though his belly crawled with tension. The stolen seal was not that well hidden. If Delvinia, like some women he had known, developed a spurt of energy after the initial exhaustion following sex play, decided to do some business, and missed that seal . . . When Max's relief finally came, Max staggered straight ahead instead of turning right in the corridor, fumbled behind the first tapestry he came to, and stumbled halfway down the stairs. There he sat down, leaned against the wall, and began to employ the techniques he knew for concentrated rest and relaxation.

A short time later, Max felt his way down the remainder of the stairs into the silent, empty Hall of the Red Larth. The green moonlight, filtered through leaves stirred by the night breeze, touched the soaring pillars and muralled walls erratically so that the blazing crimson dragon shapes seemed to quiver into alertness. Jeweled eyes glittered suddenly and winked out. Max hesitated, chiding himself for irrational nervousness, but was quite unable to move out into the room.

Then, something gibbered in the dark. Max froze, flattening himself against the wall. He did not dare move down behind the tapestry lest the movement attract attention, and he stood as rigid as any of the statuary that ornamented the Hall. It was so silent in the huge chamber now that Max could hear his heart pounding. A few more heartbeats and he let the breath he had been holding trickle out. That sound must have been another trick of his imagination, perhaps the call of a flying thing or an animal in the park outside. Nonetheless, he slid cautiously behind the tapestry and sidled away toward the center of the wall where a split between two hangings would permit him to be clear of the door and still examine the room before he stepped out.

As his eyes grew more accustomed to the dark, Max gained confidence. There was a faint, faint susurrus, but surely that was the sound of his own breathing. Still he waited, staring into the Hall where green moonlight made crimson dragons purple-black, stir softly, and watch with a shifting glitter of eye. But no darker shadow moved within the shadow. Nothing but moonlight came and went in the Hall. Max shrugged, annoyed with himself because Delvinia's incipient madness and his sense of guilt over filching the seal (not to mention his worry about what would happen to anyone Delvinia suspected of taking it, if she noticed) had thrown him so far off balance. He raised a hand to put aside the tapestry.

A wailing shriek, half agony, half maniacal laughter went off right in his ear. Max's head snapped right, his hands rose to strike—but there was nothing there. For a single heartbeat he wondered whether he was going mad; for another, he wondered whether this world had real supernatural beings. Before he had a chance at a third, equally reasonable, guess, the tapestry to his right pulled and fluttered. Something darted from behind it in a crouching scuttle to disappear behind a pillar.

However unpleasant the apparition, Max was relieved. Some pet animal escaped and frightened probably. The gibbous lob shrieked like that when angry, although they were much smaller. But the shadows in the room might have given the impression of size. Max knew he could not linger. He had only a few bell-tenths and a tremendous area to search. Nonetheless, he hesitated. The creature was gibbering again from behind the pillar and to move out into the Hall might set it off shrieking. The walls of these chambers were thick, but the passages echoed. Such shrieks might easily be heard and bring investigators.

As if his thought had drawn them, Max heard voices. These too sounded right in his ear, and Max's breath caught until he realized that the sound was coming down a second stairwell and bouncing sideways toward him from the tight-woven tapestry. Cautiously he shrank back a little from his crack, but not so far he could not see.

Three at least were hurrying down the stairwell, their voices raised in recrimination or excitement. The creature in the Hall heard them too and burst into a torrent of shrieks that sent a chill down Max's spine. There was a note of rage in those sounds that was somehow unanimal. A gleam of torchlight lit the space between tapestry and wall briefly. Max froze, but the light passed swiftly as the torchbearer swept the hanging back to enter the main chamber.

Now Max could see the pevi, and his lips formed in a soundless hiss. That was some "pet"! Torchlight gleamed on bloodstained faces and arms. Both fangs and claws had been at work. Thanks be to Yelth and Trolg that whatever it was had not sensed him. Less fearful of being noticed because he was sure the three pursuers would be too busy with their escapee to pay attention to anything else, Max pressed closer to his crack.

As the light advanced the thing dashed from behind the pillar to the huge double doors leading to the passage that connected the Hall of the Red Larth with the Grand Hall. He heard the bar that held it shut creak as the creature either pulled or pushed at the doors. When they did not give, another series of shrieks tore the air. Max's breath caught again. That was no animal! Words were mixed in the screams and gibberish. Max could not help but be sorry for the poor hunted thing although he realized that it could not be allowed to run around loose. When it could not open the doors, it turned and, still screaming, charged. For one long moment before it leaped, animallike, upon one of the pevi, Max saw it clearly. He shrank back, swallowing sickly.

Delvinia, much younger and one step further down the path to madness, could be this thing's twin. The cascade of golden hair, tumbled and knotted, the perfect features twisted in rage, the gleaming eyes bulging with total insanity. Max bit his lip. A Bolvan guard and a Bralidom of unusual size were grappling with the poor mad creature. At first Max was surprised by how long it was taking them to subdue it, but then he realized that none of them would strike the mad female or even grip it hard enough to raise a bruise. The torchbearer was darting in and out, holding a long swathe of cloth. At last the Bolvan caught it across the creature's body and, in a few moments, the captive was securely wrapped and helpless.

The shrieks were now of such volume that Max instinctively put his hands to his ears, although the gesture had little value because his helmet was in the way. The Bralidom, who Max now saw was also female, spoke softly, soothingly. Quite suddenly the shrieks changed to wild laughter and then drifted into inane giggling.

"Let us be gone from here," the Bolvan said impatiently in Enthok.

"Shut your mouth, you fool," the Bralidom hissed. "Do you want to carry her shrieking through the corridors so that Sinkek may know his daughter has escaped again?"

"No, of course not, but we are right under the royal wing. Someone may have already heard."

The torchbearer nodded in nervous agreement to this and the Bralidom hissed impatiently but returned to her soothing murmurs. Then she teased open the drooling lips and tipped the contents of a small vial into the mouth. The torchbearer drew a sharp breath.

"You will use that water weed once too often on her," the pev muttered.

Soon even the giggles stilled. The mad creature

drooped in the Bolvan's arms and was transferred to
the Bralidom's. Max watched the sad little procession
cross the Hall and disappear up the stairs behind the
tapestry. He found that he was shuddering and could
not stop. If all of Sinkek's children were like this poor
briska, it was no wonder Sinkek wished to mix his
genes with the most distant strain possible. Sinkek
wished? What could Sinkek know of genetics? Kole
had said—yes, Max remembered that clearly enough
—Sinkek had been told to raise up such a Drail. And
Delvinia had mentioned a name—Bithe. Again there
was the stirring of—of what? Implanted ideas? Max
waited for revelation, but none came. The key to his
purpose had not yet been put into his hand.

He waited a little longer to be sure no one would
come to investigate the noise. Then, no longer concerned by the ghostly appearance of movement among
the sculpted and painted larths in the wake of the real
horrors he had seen, Max made his way swiftly across
to the double doors that had frustrated the mad Drail.
Instead of the sliding latch common to the smaller
doors of the palace, this had a lever mechanism that
lifted the heavier bar necessary. Max felt a twinge of
anxiety as he pressed down that the door would be
locked, but the bar lifted readily and, indeed, locking
would be purposeless as the connecting corridor led
only to the Grand Hall.

When the doors were closed, the corridor beyond
was pitch black. Max felt his way along until he found
the door. This time he did not pause to let his imagination give life to the great murals. He darted across the
vast moonlit chamber, listened a moment, and then
opened the doors and slipped into another black
passageway.

The Hall of the Seven Cities had been built generations earlier in a period of unusual amity. Here the murals were great illustrated maps, three to each long wall and one at each end. Max did not linger, but he was aware of the utter silence. The walls of these older chambers were thicker, he guessed, and the smaller windows cut down on both light and sound. The doors were not opposite in this Hall but at the north end, because the Hall of the Great Sea, a still older edifice, lay behind.

Now Max was in the totally unused portion of the palace. Dust lay thick on the floors. The scenes of shipping and fishing and sea battles were dim and flaking, and the moonlight scarcely distinguished the formalized wave-pattern carving on the pillars. Max cursed the dimness softly. He was sharply aware of the passage of time and his inability to see well hindered his search. Each pillar in each Hall was surrounded by candle sconces, and Max hoped that a few in this old Hall retained candles. He did not like to take any from the Halls in use lest someone notice they were gone and wonder who was unofficially wandering around in the dark.

Gritting his teeth with impatience, Max forced himself to search until he found three. Fortunately they were very large candles. They would have to do; he could not afford to spend any more time. Then for a few sickening moments he could not find a door behind the hangings. He cursed himself softly. He had become disoriented. This was the west wall of the westmost Hall; of course, there would be no doors. He recrossed the Hall and found a hanging. Handling it with ginger gentleness, for the cloth was dry to the point of tattering, Max slid behind it and felt along. The door lever he eventually found was stiff with disuse. Max bit his lips as he worked at it, terrified that these old passages might have been sealed off for safety's sake, but it yielded at last.

In the black of the stairwell, Max opened his belt pouch and felt for the smaller pouch within. From this he drew a small metal box containing tinder, which he opened, and two small firestones. Steadily, despite his impatience, using the light of the sparks to guide him, he struck, blew, held the candle wick to the tiny flame. As it caught he heard himself muttering, and grinned. He had been saying, "Come on, Yelth, get this thing lit." It was nice to have a god to call on, whether you believed in it or not.

Somehow the golden glow was comforting, however little actual light it gave. Max mounted the stairs with confidence, reassured by the cebar-thick dust that muffled his footsteps. The door at the top was also stiff but, his impatience less, Max made much quicker work of opening it. Shielding his light, he peered through a tiny crack before he opened the door wide enough to step through. The corridor was not inviting. Black as the entrance to Trolg's domain, it smelled of disuse and ancient death.

Once again Max checked his unruly imagination and set out to the left along the cross corridor. All the doors were closed but Max did not try any of them because they were the wide, ornamented portals of living chambers. Kole had said the Enthok female was imprisoned on the third level, and Max was looking for a way up. At the end of the corridor, he slowed, listening, but only the silence of ages assaulted his ears. He turned the corner and trotted quickly north. One wall was completely blank, which told Max he was at the westernmost end of the complex again. The other wall showed the customary doorways. Max opened two, but both stairwells led down.

The fourth living-quarter door that he passed was open and attracted Max's eye as he trotted past. Three bars down the corridor he paused and reversed his steps. There had been furniture in that room. A sharp memory of Delvinia's furnishings gave him an idea. To rescue Zabulin (if he was worth rescuing) would require money or some other medium of bribery. Perhaps something of value had been left in one of the chambers. A swift examination of the room brought a low hiss of satisfaction from him. The apartment had been rifled, true, but the gouges and tears showed where gems and gold wire had been ruthlessly removed. It would not take much more time to check for another furnished room.

Now Max briefly opened each door he passed. To his disappointment, all the rooms seemed empty. At the cross corridor, Max turned right again. Here there were doors both left and right, but to his dismay every stairwell led down. He was sure Kole had pointed out at least two that led upward in the inhabited section. At the end of this cross corridor, he turned left again and moved north. He was now above the Hall of the Seven Battles, the second oldest of the Great Halls. Still he found only empty, dust-blanketed rooms and down stairways. The corridor ended in a great window and a cross corridor without any doors at all. It was possible, Max realized with a sinking heart, that the old Halls never had a third level.

Max turned left automatically, while he considered whether he should go down and try for the third level in the inhabited section upon some excuse. He could see the blank end of this corridor and was just about to turn and try this new, more dangerous course, when a chilly breeze raised bumps on his skin. But the window had not been open. Ahead, a single sagging door stood ajar. Max looked in and drew a deep breath. A twisting stair at last led upward. Two steps up, Max stumbled on fallen masonry. It was the first sign of decay he had found in spite of the obvious neglect of this section of the palace. He climbed more carefully in spite of his eagerness, slid through another half-open sagging door at the top, and bit back an exclamation of frustration. This certainly did not lead to any section on the third level.

He was in a round tower room which seemed to be an excrescence on the building rather than an integral part of it. A watch tower? But why so neglected and unmanned? Max shivered in the chill night breeze and looked at the large window. Not a defensive tower then, with a window rather than arrow- and observation-slits. He shrugged; no matter how interesting the problem he had no time to try to solve it. Turning to leave, his foot struck a decayed mass on the floor. Lowering his candle solved the puzzle. However cultures differed and however decayed, the forms of a tripod and telescope were unmistakable. Doubtless the tower had been built for some noble stargazer.

As he came down the stairs, Max wondered how. He had seen no evidence of cantilevered construction, even among the technologically more advanced Bralidom. Behind the open door of the tower stairs was the answer—another door, which had been hidden, furnished with three enormous bars on the corridor side. The area Max looked into when he had levered the bars off and worked the door open was long and narrow. Beyond the floor of the tower, it was open above to the sky, and slits broke the outer wall, which was taller than his head. This then must be where the palace wall met the city wall. Max believed there would be a door at the other end, although he could

not see it, but he did not go out at first. Doubtless that
far door would also be barred on the corridor inside.
The purpose of the bars was now clear too. They
would prevent, or at least delay, any attacker from
entering the body of the palace. They could be used
for a crueler purpose too. If the defenders were sealed
into the area, they would fight very hard to repel an
invader.

But that was very long in the past, going back to
the days before Enthok fought as mercenaries. That
reminded Max. Grimly he counted arrow slits. In the
center slit he jammed one of his precious candles cross-
wise. It would not be noticeable to a casual glance, he
hoped, but if he succeeded in rescuing Jael he would
have a marker for Clan Vinci that would show an
open door into Sinkek's stronghold. The next step was
to close the door firmly and to carry away the three
bars to be concealed in various rooms in the next cross
corridor.

When that was traversed, Max turned left yet again.
This should take him to the area that covered the
oldest Hall of all, named simply, Old Hall. He sighed
with relief when the corridor showed the familiar
triply barred door. These bars Max also removed and
hid. Elated with this piece of serendipity, he was suddenly gifted with a brilliant idea.

Xers and Ptar had seen Jael in a tower window of
the city wall. Max now knew that one tower had been
built on the northwest side. He would lay odds that
another had been built to the southeast to give the
stargazer a complete view of the heavens. What that
tower had been built on originally, Max could not
guess; possibly atop the wall which, at that time, had
not been connected to the palace. Then when the new,
three-level hall was added, the old city wall was used

and the tower simply became part of the new third level.

Max trotted rapidly down the corridor. Then, pausing to orient himself, his eye was caught by another door barred from the outside. This barred door, however, was something else. The bar was no part of the original door. Another door, hung so that it opened outward had been set over the first. Not quite knowing why he did so, Max lifted, but the bar resisted. With a growing sense of horror, he saw the bar was wedged shut. Quickly he lowered his candle. The dust seemed just as thick here as elsewhere. Nonetheless, he could not take so desperate a chance as to ignore a room obviously devised to retain a prisoner. Consigning Sinkek and all his family, too, to the worst torments of Trolg's many hells, Max worked the wedges free with his dagger, lifted the bar, cursed once again, and opened the door.

No pitiful form, arms outstretched for release that never came, blocked the doorway. Only a miasma of old, old death seeped out. Max choked, but he knew this was no stench of putrefaction—only the moldering of organic matter untouched for untold ages. He almost retreated, then realized the room was completely furnished. Maybe here he would find a bauble to trade for Zabulin. To his disappointment the chairs and tables were plain. The handles and pulls of doors and drawers that he rubbed free of dust were beautifully carved, but only of wood. Curiosity and a feeling that he must not waste this opportunity overcame reluctance, and Max moved toward the inner rooms.

The flickering light showed first the huge, curtained bed, but the hangings had rotted to a frayed tatter or two and Max could see dimly into it. Propped on pillows lay a thing, part mummy, part skeleton, its head

90

turned as if the black hollows where eyes had once been could see who had disturbed the eons-long silence. This was no prisoner who had died in despair. The lower part of the face was hidden by some material that had, presumably, bound the lax jaw shut. Only the huge, empty eye sockets showed. The arms lay restfully beside the body. Max could see no hands but assumed the bones had been swallowed up in the dust that lay so thickly on the rich counterpane that no color could be seen. That covering lay perfectly smooth over the slight, slight bulge of the desiccated body. No dying being could lie so still; that cover had been smoothed after the breath of life was gone.

Nothing could be seen in the polished oval of silver that had served as a mirror because of the blackening of ages and the pall of dust that clung to it. Max considered it briefly, but its weight and size made concealment impossible despite its value. A few unfamiliar-looking toilet articles, the soft parts long rotted away, lay on the dressing table undisturbed. Quickly Max examined them. They were gold, but also large and marked with what Max was sure was a distinctive pattern. Still, if there was nothing else . . .

But there was! A lump in the dust made Max lower his candle and garb. His thumb rubbed across a smooth stone. Flame glinted at him—a ruby! Hastily he opened drawers and gasped—rings, necklets, armlets. Everything this pev, or more likely Drail or Zel, had owned was here. Max had Zabulin's ransom ten times over. Nonetheless, his hand hesitated. He glanced over his shoulder.

"Zel," he said softly, half ashamed but unable to resist the urge to placate the still form, "I am sorry to rob you, but you will never need them again and they will be used for the good of a distant descendent of yours and, I think, of all the people of this city."

The armlets he ignored; the rings he took wholesale; and he wrenched those gems held only by delicate prongs from the necklets. Then, reverently, he bowed and retreated, carefully rebarring and wedging the mysterious door.

Chapter 8

Now Max retraced his steps to the area over the Hall of the Silver Arrow. To his relief he soon found an up stair, indicating that the third level went back at least this far. The corridor into which the door at the top of the stairs opened was dark and still, probably unoccupied. Silently he crept along the corridor until a faint gleam made him extinguish his candle. To his intense relief, the corridor he arrived at was empty, although well-enough lit with hanging oil lamps. Kole had spoken truly when he said there would be few guards because it was occupied largely by servants.

Max slipped his sandals off and ran the full length of the corridor as fast and as silently as possible. At the corner he peeped out. Clear! He almost started again and then cursed softly. Opposite end, stupid, he told himself. This tower would be right, not left. Then his breath caught. He had been lucky. A slender, richly dressed Bralidom rounded the corner far to the left and walked stealthily in Max's direction.

Shrinking back, Max flattened himself against the wall and hoped. Second time lucky. The Bralidom knocked at and entered a door before he came abreast of Max. Probably a young noble visiting where he had no right to be. All to the good. That was one more person who would not be able to explain where he was this night. Now the corridor was clear and Max took it at a run. The short corridor leading to the passage that ran along the back city–palace wall was clear also. Just before he came to this last corner, Max paused to steady his breathing. Then he crouched and literally crept to the corner. A pev on watch naturally looks at pev's height for intruders. Stealthily, his head only inches from the floor, Max peered out.

He would have sighed with relief had he not been afraid to make even that kind of sound. The tower door was there, it was barred on the corridor side, and a guard was stationed in front of it. Someone, therefore, was a prisoner in the tower room. Max sat back on his heels and considered how he could draw the guard toward him, since the distance was too far for him to cover before an alarm could be given. Noises were out. Any unusual noise would cause the guard to summon help. Max glanced uneasily over his shoulder. He could not afford to make any sound that would penetrate the doors or he would have everyone out in the corridor. Max drew his knife and rubbed the blade along the edge of the wall.

"Come on, Yelth and Trolg," he mouthed silently. "Make him curious." For a while, however, it seemed as if Gorona's gods felt they had been cooperative enough. The next little scraping noise Max made brought the Bolvan's head around. He frowned and looked in the other direction. Max held his breath, but made a briefer scratching. The guard stiffened as if he were about to call out, then he turned and started to walk in Max's direction. When he was a few steps away, Max threw one of the rings he had filched at a diagonal so that it fell behind the Bolvan. One instant later, he was out in a single leap and his hand had caught the back of the guard's neck, just under the flare of the helmet.

The Bolvan dropped like a stunned bullock between step and step. Max was too off balance to catch him and he fell heavily, with a thud that made Max freeze. Then he caught up the unconscious pev, ran back the few steps to the door of the tower. Here he dropped his victim as much as possible in the shadow of the doorway and stood in front of him. If anyone had heard the thud and came to look, a hasty glance would show only a Bolvan standing guard.

Max counted one hundred bell-thousandths and then another, but no one came. He untied the guard's sandals, bound his arms behind him and his ankles together, and gagged him. Then, cautiously, he unbarred the door and opened it just a trifle. There was a short corridor, probably covering what had been the top of the city wall, leading to another door. Max brought the guard in, closed the door, took his victim's weapons in hand.

"Open up," Max called, adding the password of the changing guard.

There was a short silence, the sound of stirring. "Open it yourself," a beautiful voice replied with a hint of malice under sleepiness.

Max tried the lever and the latch clicked. The door was not locked. He hesitated for a moment. A guard would not dare sleep and there had been malice in that invitation. But no one could possibly guess he was an unofficial visitor. Then whoever answered did not welcome visitors. Jael herself? Max had waited long enough after the lock clicked to put any one expecting the door to open at once slightly off guard. Now he slammed the door back with all the strength he had and leaped forward into the room.

He almost escaped the trap, but not quite. A basin, precariously balanced between two long rods and the door emptied a quart of liquid over him. The rods flew back striking a table with a resounding whack, the basin fell with an incredible clatter, and the most beautiful being Max had ever seen—without flattery—laughed uproariously.

Another leap put Max's back against a wall, but the room was empty except for the laughing goddess, who, for all her mirth, had a sword in one hand and a most efficient dagger ready for throwing in the other. Max dropped the guard's weapons which he was carrying and hastily raised his empty hands.

"Will the noise draw someone?" he gasped.

"Not from this tower," Jael replied, still laughing and watching him warily.

"Jael, Ptar said that the rock upon which you cut your foot on the bank of the Gelv Gibbous Lob had golden flecks, and the three parts into which Pev Goloth split it were buried with him."

The laughter stopped as suddenly as if a door had slammed shut upon it. The beautifully shaped, glossy black lips remained slightly parted, the luminous silver eyes showed hope struggling with caution. "Was there any other word for Jael?" the Thal whispered.

"Xers said that yellow fibbil were not sweet to eat even when they were stolen fruit."

A tiny smile softened the tenseness of Jael's expression, but she checked the happy memory. "Who are you, Bolvan?"

"My name is Max." He drew his own sword and dagger, saw her tense, but threw them wide of her onto the bed. "I will tell you everything you want to know, but come away from here now. We must escape before we talk. It has taken me far too long to get here. The guard must be due to change soon."

In a heartbeat she had decided. She sheathed her own weapons and took Max's in hand. "Come away from the arms," she said, and Max stepped clear of the guard's weapons without attempting to pick them up. What he did pick up was the unconscious guard, whom he dumped into Jael's bed. She nodded as he removed the helmet, shoved it behind a chair, and drew the covers up over the pev's head. Then Max blew out the oil lamps, gathered three, all he could hold in one hand and arm, and drew the door shut behind him. After he opened the corridor door a crack to be sure the passage was still clear, he said, "Down the corridor to the left, then down the first door behind a tapestry. It does not matter which door."

Jael gestured with the sword. "You lead."

Max opened the door wider, slipped out, and when Jael had passed him, rebarred the door. Perhaps the guard who came on duty would not report his fellow guard immediately if there did not seem to be anything amiss. It was not likely, but he might at least wait a few minutes, and every minute would help.

The empty corridors were traversed. Max pulled aside the hanging that shielded the stairwell door. Just before he stepped in, he ignited his candle at an oil lamp nearby. When the door shut behind them, Max drew his lungs full of air. It felt like the first breath he had taken since he hit the guard.

"We must go down again," Max whispered. "We can cross through the Great Halls to the Hall of the Seven Battles. I know the second level there is deserted. Then we can talk."

"Why not escape from the city altogether?" Jael's hands tensed on her weapons as suspicion swept her.

"There is no time. For miles around the city there is only farmland, no place to hide, and it will soon be light. The farmers this close to the city are terrified of Sinkek. They will help no one, nor do they welcome strangers. Besides, the city gates are locked at night. There is no way out, save one, and I have not what is needful to escape that way."

The soft, rich voice spat an oath, but Jael's grip on Max's weapons relaxed. "Although I have been pent in that stone hell, I forgot the city walls."

No answer was necessary, and Max carefully lifted the latch and eased out into the tapestry-shielded entrance to the Hall of the Red Eyes of Trolg. Jael slipped silently to his side. As Max lifted the tapestry, Jael's breath hissed inward softly. The moons, which had been in the southwest when Max started his search, were low in the northeast now. Green moonslight, if not as bright as in the Hall of the Red Larth, was still bright enough to illuminate the mural that covered the opposite wall. Max paused too for a moment's admiration, and then did a double take.

The scene was not one any pev could ever have seen. It was in fact an aerial, or rather a near-space, view, showing at the bottom, hugely, the curve of Gorona and above, lurid in the silver-green light, the two red moons with their silver-pink prisoner between. Suppressing his desire to examine the scene more closely and to ask why Jael had gasped at sight of it, Max hurried across the empty chamber. At the double doors, he handed Jael the candle, which she grasped in two long fingers without releasing her grip on the knife. Then, patiently, Max set himself to work the rusted levers that would give egress from the Hall of the Red Eyes of Trolg. When they had made their way through the Old Hall into the Hall of the Seven Battles, Max stopped. This chamber had been so long unused that the hangings were dry and frail. Nonetheless he drew Jael behind one and turned to face her.

"Thal, I believe you will be safe here for a little while. The palace is so huge, and much of it is unused and empty. I think, unless every pev of the guard is called out, that you could hide in the upper chambers for weeks."

"But," Jael protested softly, her eyes bleak, "Sinkek will call out the whole guard. He may think my people are all dead——" Her voice faltered.

"No, no." Max hastened to offer comfort. "There were heavy losses, but the clan is intact. Xers is unhurt and Ptar is recovering well. Your briski too are well and safe."

She smiled her gratitude but did not ask for details, a piece of self-control Max admired. Instead she said, "This mad Zel thinks he has other uses for me than hostage. He will take down the palace stone by stone if he guesses I am in it."

Max grinned. "That is our one chance—that he should not guess. I will try to strike down the pev who guards the entrance doors and lay a trail to one of the water gates to make it seem you have escaped into a boat."

Jael nodded immediate acceptance and proffered Max's weapons. "Go," she said. "I will wait here or, if someone comes, I will slip into the stairs behind us. If

I am driven out to the floors above, I will return here when I can."

"It is easy to lose oneself," Max cautioned.

Jael smiled, a benign, gently amused goddess, silver touched with gilt from the candle flame. "I will blaze a trail so that none but I will notice the marks. Go."

"Give me that," Max said, pointing to a decorative seal that adorned Jael's dagger sheath, and she looked questioning but pressed it into his hand.

The first part of Max's program was simple. Palace guards were alert enough to keep thieves and assassins out; but they scarcely expected to be attacked from within. The guard at the main entrance to the Hall of the Seven Cities was rendered unconscious and dragged off into a convenient nearby clump of bushes without the slightest difficulty. Max was far more cautious in approaching the outer wall. Because of the war games Sinkek had his men play, the gate guards were very wary and alert to any movement both inside and outside.

Fortunately, there was a small water gate that led to the royal docks as well as the huge gates that were opened to welcome official visitors who came by sea. The smaller gate, a convenience for those who wished to go pleasure sailing, was guarded as carefully as the larger—more carefully, perhaps—but Max knew he could never unbar the great gates without help. Flat on his belly, he inched along behind a formal flower bed to its end. It was the only cover he could find and it ended some twenty bars from the wall.

Moonslight was low behind him. This was an advantage in that it made the guards visible; it also would silhouette Max starkly if he so much as lifted his head. Max felt around in the flower bed and soon had a handful of pebbles. Rolling to his side he flung one at the wall. It was not a large pebble and made only the faintest click as it hit. Nonetheless, both guards looked in the direction of the sound. Max threw another so that it hit the wall a little higher. Both guards backed away so that they could see the top of the wall. Each then made a quick scan along the inside of the wall and the nearby garden, but the treeless and shrubless expanse did not seem able to conceal anything that could make the noise. Finally they looked for a few expectant moments at the top of the wall again.

One never knew what hit him. The other had a chance to utter a single choked cry as his companion fell. He did not, Max was sure, have a chance to turn his head and identify his attacker as a Bolvan guard before he was felled. Leaving the two where they lay, Max thrust up the bar of the smaller gate and shoved it open. Halfway under it he placed Jael's seal. It was not the best place, but a voice from the great gate had already called a question. There was now time for no more but concealment.

In fact, Max was barely belly down beside the flower bed again before one of the guards from the main water gate came quickly though stealthily along the wall, sword in hand. Max pressed as close to the tall stems as possible without touching them and wriggled forward as frantically as he could. At the end of the bed, he paused, gasping with effort and wondering whether his fatigue was dimming his sight. Then he grinned. This life of adventure was hard on the nerves. The dimness was not his eyes but moonsset.

When the guard's shout indicated that he had found the unconscious pevi or the open gate, Max rose to a runner's crouch. With the moons down it was less likely that a glitter from his harness or the movement of his shadow would give him away, although the red eyes of Trolg still glared a dull and lurid light. As he saw the guard stoop, he scuttled to a clump of ornamental bushes. From there cover was better and Max soon slipped in the great entrance doors, which he closed carefully but did not bar.

Eventually he was back in the Hall of the Seven Battles. No light. Not a whisper of sound. Had they been searching already? Cautiously, he sidled to the wall, felt his way along it, trying to remember which stair Jael said she would retreat to. Halfway along, Max stopped suddenly, the cold, sharp point of a sword at his throat just under the curving guard of the helmet. It was a very clever move, the sword pointing in through the opening in the tapestry made it impossible to get at the person holding it. Max waited one long bell-thousandth and then chuckled.

"It is I, Max," he whispered. "Let me come out. I can stay but a moment. It will be morning bell soon and I must report back."

The sword dropped and Max stepped out at once. He could see nothing, but Jael's voice came from right in front of him, disapprovingly. "You are not very cautious."

Max chuckled again. "Yes I am. I waited for you to challenge me, as any Bolvan guard would. Even a Bralidom would have cried out an alarm. But first take these jewels—I will tell you how I came by them when there is more time." He fumbled for her hand blindly until she took the pouch from him. To Max the darkness was absolute, but apparently Jael could still see a little. "I must go," he repeated. "I will return here after midnight bell tomorrow—I hope—and bring food and water. I do not believe I dare come sooner."

"Do not trouble for me." Jael's silvery voice was calm and assured. "I am fed full. I can do without eating for three days at least and I think I know where water is to be found. If not, I will make shift to do without. I will be here each night after midnight bell. Do not be troubled if you cannot come tomorrow."

Chapter 9

Max returned as far as the Hall of the Red Larth. Moonslight gone, the dragons returned to immobility, and Max tried not to remember what else he had seen. On the side opposite the doors that eventually led outside to the Bolvan quarters, he lay down on the floor behind a tapestry near the wall. Still near to trembling with excitement, he never expected to sleep, but he had had a long, hard day. Sometime later he was dimly aware of light beyond his eyelids and shouts and pounding feet, but sleep swallowed him again and he did not stir until a foot was applied ungently to his ribs. Rising with a gasp of surprise, he saw two Bolvi guards, swords drawn, staring down at him. Max rubbed his side ruefully.

"Up," one said.

Max slid out from under the tapestry that the other was holding and rose. "You need not draw sword on me," he remarked pacifically. "I am more than willing to come out of this maze."

When it was clear they were marching him outside, Max's well-concealed tenseness began to ebb. Had he been really suspected or had Jael been recaptured, he would have been taken either directly to the torture room below or to Sinkek's quarters for questioning. Instead he faced the Manili who had enlisted him. That too was good. He knew Max as a foreigner, unlikely to have any connection with dissident nobles or northern clans of Enthok.

"Why were you asleep in the Hall of the Red Larth?"

The question was sharp with authority, but Max noted that his weapons had not been confiscated and that the Manili made an impatient gesture to dismiss the other Bolvi. Max grinned deprecatingly, shuffled his feet, and fluttered his hands in a helpless, embarrassed way.

"I was lost, Manili," he replied with an awkward half laugh. But he slid his eyes away from the gold-green gaze of his officer.

"Lost? Kole showed you the chambers, did he not?" That was sharper, showing that the Manili had picked up Max's uneasy, guilty glance.

Max repeated the fluttering gesture of the hands and the awkward laugh. "I was sleepy and I must have gone down the wrong stair. The Hall looked all different in the moonslight too." Max paused. His grin disappeared. "The larths—they—they seemed to move. In my hurry to leave that place, I must have gone out the wrong door."

The Manili's brow ridges rose in a most human expression of sarcastic doubt. "And you were wandering about bell-tenth after bell-tenth until, quite by accident, you found your way back to the Hall of the Red Larth, and you were so exhausted you just curled up to go to sleep?" The brows dropped, the sarcastic sneer was replaced by a threatening scowl, the tone changed from a drawl to a roar. "You are lying. The most important prisoner in the palace has escaped! Where have you been?"

"Escaped?" Max gasped. "But they caught her again, I—" And he raised a hand to cover his mouth as if he had been startled into saying more than he intended.

The Manili's eyes bulged. He reached across the table and caught Max by the strap of his harness. "Who caught her? Where? Quickly!"

"I—" Max hesitated, as if unwilling.

"Will you tell me now, or would you prefer to tell them in the torture chamber?"

Max jerked back indignantly. "I have done nothing wrong. I thought what I saw was no affair of mine, and I do not like to tell other pevi's secrets, but it is nothing to me worth being racked over. A Bolvan guard and two Bralidom females recaptured her in the Hall of the Red Larth. I saw them go up the stair to the level above. More than that I do not know."

"A Bolvan guard and two Bralidom females?" The Manili sounded stunned. "What Bolvan guard?"

"I do not know him. Not so tall as I. His sword leather was bossed in silver. I remember the torchlight gleaming on it. One Bralidom female was huge— bigger than I am. She was not armed. The other was smaller. I do not remember anything special about her. A very ordinary female servant."

"And she went willingly with them?"

"Willingly!" Max exclaimed with a shudder. "She tore them with teeth and nails. They bled, face and arms, before they caught her in a cloth and bound her softly."

The Manili shook his head as if what Max was saying was making him dizzy. "She did not fight with a sword?"

"A sword?" Max nearly shrieked. "Who would give such a one a sword?" He shuddered again. "I will not serve here for any price if that Drail comes to rule."

"What?"

Max dropped his voice almost to a whisper and leaned forward. "I could not help but hear. The big Bralidom said it was Sinkek's briska. It is no wonder he prisons her close."

"Sinkek's briska?" The Manili's expression of eager interest was replaced by one of fear and distaste. His voice too was lowered. "So she was loose again, eh? She is slyer than . . . That was not the prisoner of whom I spoke."

Max looked first bland and then a little disgusted. "You mean more than *one* prisoner escaped last night?"

The Manili bristled a bit at the implied criticism. His voice was cold when he asked, "You saw nothing else?"

"That was quite enough," Max replied, hunching his shoulders with reminiscent revulsion. "It seemed to me then better to stay where I was until daylight. If that thing burst down again . . . Besides, if none had asked, it was safer not to know such a thing." Then he cocked his head. "Who was the other escaped prisoner?"

"An Enthok female. You will be well rewarded if you hear anything. . . . Sometimes a guard outside a door hears things."

"I knew there was an Enthok female," Max said

slowly. "Kole mentioned that the Zel had such a prisoner. But how could she escape? An Enthok in a city —or do your northern Enthok visit the cities?"

"They do not, and it would be hard to hide her. She will be sought even under the stones." There was a definite warning in that which Max could not understand. It was not directed at him personally. If he had been suspected even slightly at any time he would have been in the torture chamber now. The Manili paused significantly, frowned at Max's openly questioning look, and continued. "There are jealousies and feuds among the Great Ones that are no business of ours. Your duty is simply to report at once if you see or hear anything that might lead to the Enthok. Remember, no matter what *anyone* promises, the Zel has more to give—and more power to take away."

Anyone? The emphasis was significant. Delvinia was obviously suspected. Then he might be under suspicion after all—bait to catch Delvinia. He made no response to the Manili's remark beyond the fist to chest gesture and head bob that comprised the local salute. Receiving in reply a wave of dismissal, Max went off to get something to eat and then to his little room to finish his interrupted sleep. It was very necessary to act in a perfectly normal manner. He removed his clothing and sandals, fastened the stolen seal more securely into his hair knot, and, in spite of renewed tenseness, dropped off to sleep almost as soon as he hit the bed.

He was not to catch up on lost sleep, however. Max was wakened by a thunderous knocking at his door what seemed moments after he closed his eyes. He was out of bed, defensively crouched, before he gathered enough wakefulness to ask who it was.

"By order of the Manili," was the response.

"What order?" Max growled, swallowing his heart and keeping his voice thick, as if he were still half asleep.

"Early duty. Hurry."

Although it might have been a trap, Max was reassured. If something had gone wrong, why would the guard knock? Surely then a group would have tried to rush in without warning and overpower him before he could get to his weapons. "I come," Max responded.

He was further reassured when the door did not open while he flung on his kilt and harness, strapped on his weapons, and grabbed his cloak. However, the expression on the Manili's face—an officer with whom Max was not familiar—betokened some kind of trouble. The glance from his lion-brown eyes held contempt and, perhaps, a warning.

"You are summoned to a half-duty extra to guard Drail Delvinia." The voice was cold and remote. "Half elef extra will be added to your wage."

There was a pause. Max, not knowing how to respond, simply waited. Then, because the officer said nothing else, and his expression did not invite questions, Max started to salute. An impatient hiss drew his attention.

"The guard on duty went mad, it seems, and offered violence and insult to the Drail. It was necessary for her—or for her servants, it is not clear which—to kill him to defend her."

Max's mouth opened, then closed slowly into a hard line. It was not beyond the bounds of remote possibility that this was true. Max would soon know, because Delvinia's apartment would be a shambles and most of her servants dead or wounded. An armed and enraged Bolvan would mow down a rabble of Bralidom servants like hay. Otherwise, Delvinia had murdered that young Bolvan. Max saluted sharply and received his pass from the Manili. As soon as he was outside, he examined it carefully. It had been taken, ready prepared, from a slot and he could see no difference between this and the one Kole had used. Whether it was good always or only until sunrise bell, Max was not sure, but that should be long enough provided Delvinia did not keep him beyond midnight. Max thought of the young guard and his resolution hardened. He turned toward the latrine instead of toward the palace. In the uncared-for area behind it he thought he had seen waterweed. Delvinia would sleep soundly tonight —very soundly.

There was no guard at Delvinia's door, and Max knocked on it very softly. A servant, neat and showing not the smallest evidence of damage or excitement, opened the door at once. "My apologies to the noble one, if I disturbed her," Max whispered. "I did not know whether I was supposed to report myself. I am on duty now by order of the Manili."

He made to show his pass, but the servant did not look at it, merely nodded and closed the door. Max was a little disappointed. He had rather expected to be told to come in. He had not been in guard position more than a quarter bell-tenth, however, when a resplendent Bralidom male, as emerald green as Delvinia but with less delicate features and tightly bound hair, stalked into the corridor. There was no other door, so Max drew his sword in warning. The young male drew himself up in affronted dignity—but he stopped at once.

"I am Olibep, messenger of the Zel. How dare you bar my way."

"I beg pardon, noble one," Max replied smoothly,

but without lowering his weapon. "I am a new guard. I am sure you speak the truth, yet I do not know you. I will just announce your coming to the servants of the Drail."

Still facing the messenger, Max sidled to the door and rapped on it sharply with the hilt of the dagger he had drawn. After a little while the door opened and an irritable voice asked, "What?"

"Olibep, messenger of the Zel, to speak with Drail Delvinia," Max announced, standing clear of the door but still watching the newcomer.

The servant's voice gentled appreciably, almost into an apologetic whine. "A moment, please, noble one, while I tell my mistress."

A pause ensued. "You can put up your sword," Olibep snapped. "I will not charge the door."

Max did not change his stance. "I know that, noble one, yet I dare not violate my orders, which are to guard the Drail Delvinia."

The pause lengthened. Olibep shifted his feet and scowled. Max bit his lip and mentally cursed Delvinia, who was clearly intending to annoy her brother's messenger—or was she trying to test Max? At last the door opened and Delvinia herself stepped out. She took in Olibep's annoyance and Max's stolid guard position in a single glance, which, when it touched Max, displayed a spark of approval. A test then—a test passed.

"I assume my sib wants me," Delvinia remarked. "I am ready."

"Drail Delvinia," Olibep began formally, "Zel Sinkek's message . . ."

"Did he forbid me to come to him?" Delvinia asked, her voice rising ominously.

Olibep licked his lips and Max could see the struggle in his face. Obviously he wanted to keep Delvinia away from her brother, but he had no such instructions. "No, Drail," he replied.

Delvinia hunched a shoulder at him contemptuously and sailed past. Max fell in behind, thinking she was a fool to alienate pevi so gratuitously. Kole had not taken him into the corridor in which Sinkek's apartment lay, and he soon saw why. Just beyond the turn of the cross corridor, two Bolvi stood. Max could see others only four or five bars apart all the way down the corridor, where nearly all the doors stood open. A murmur of sound indicated that the rooms were occupied and Max realized that these were probably the government offices as well as Sinkek's living quarters. The guards made no attempt to stop Delvinia, or even to question her. Apparently she had access to Sinkek whenever she wished. That was interesting. Swords were out the moment Max tried to follow, however.

"Noble one," Max called, "is it my duty to accompany you?" He was reasonably sure it was not. Sinkek's guards were doubtless responsible for security in this corridor, but Delvinia was not totally sane and this might be another test.

She took another step or two, ignoring the question, then suddenly stopped and turned. "Yes, come." And then, to the guards, "Let him pass."

"He may not pass armed, not even if *you* vouch for him, Drail," Olibep said nastily.

Before the tone—a deliberate insult, Max guessed —could prick Delvinia into saying more than she meant, he had unbuckled his harness, belt pouch and all, and handed it to one of the guards. A moment later they were through ornately decorated double doors in what was obviously a semiformal reception room. Max thought he was now seeing the ultimate in luxury, as the Great Halls were the ultimate in magnificence. The colors of the silken carpet into which his feet sank glowed brilliantly. The furniture was inlaid with gold and silver and mother-of-pearl. The courtiers themselves were equally decorative, their glittering green skins and golden hair decked in shimmering silks and flashing jewels.

But none of it had the power to hold Max's eyes. At the very end of the room, lounging in a chair with cushions embroidered in gold thread and pearls, sat— a male Delvinia. Max had some difficulty in refraining from gaping. It was true that in similiarity of skin color and hair color all upper-class Bralidom were alike, but actually they resembled each other no more closely than any group of blacks, or Orientals, or blond caucasians. The striking similarity of features among the Zel, his sister, and his daughter hinted broadly at the cause of their growing disability. The Pharaohs of ancient Egypt had disintegrated physically after breeding brother to sister for some generations. Here, the perfect bodies of Sinkek's sister and daughter hid disintegrating minds. Max took a good look at Sinkek himself, but there was no madness in those eyes or, at least, no hysteria. Monomania did not show itself in the expression in the same way.

"Where is the Enthok?" Sinkek asked softly.

Max stiffened and his stride almost checked before he realized that the question had not been addressed to him. Fortunately, every eye was fixed upon Delvinia, and Max's reaction went unnoticed. The Drail stopped dead in her tracks and stared for a moment.

"The Enthok?" she repeated, and the puzzlement in her voice was genuine. "What have I to do with her? I never approved of what you tried to do, or at least of the method you used. But once done, keeping the

Enthok was right." She glanced around the circle of nobles, her eyes resting briefly with contempt on several. "I do not seek, out of cowardice, to pacify where pacification is impossible. No, sib, I suggest you seek elsewhere for those who see profit in concealing or freeing the Enthok."

"This was a problem, believe it or not, my dear sib, that disturbed my 'loyal' council—except for a few. Had I not known you had other, private, reasons for desiring the removal of the Enthok . . . As it is, I would not have believed it of you—except that you —er—removed the Bolvan who contrived the escape this morning."

Max did not move, but suddenly he was tense again. He should not have been able to understand what they were saying. Sinkek should have been speaking in Bralidom. Was all this an elaborate play, set up for him? But that was crazy. Anything he knew could be wrenched out in the torture chamber. But for whom were Sinkek and Delvinia speaking Enthok?

"You know me better than that, oh Zel," Delvinia responded seriously. "You know that when I oppose you I do so aloud before the whole court. You know also that, no matter how strong my disapproval, when you have made a decision I never act against you. I never have and I never will."

"You never have," Sinkek agreed warily.

"I did kill the Bolvan," Delvinia stated, "but the Enthok had nothing to do with that. I did not know she was gone until the searchers came. Whatever my personal feelings, I know why you do what you do. I would never interfere with that." She hesitated and rubbed her arms with her hands, as if a chill had touched her. "The Bolvan insulted me," she went on, her voice now almost indifferent. "He was too sick

114

with the Bolvan sickness to adjust. You know that is sometimes so with the young ones."

Max saw that Sinkek was not only listening but wished to be convinced. The bond between the sibs— mates too, probably—was very tight. Perhaps that was why Sinkek only spoke of mating with Jael and had never tried very hard. Perhaps those who favored that mating were trying to forward it by reducing Delvinia's influence. Max looked from one to the other. It would be like making love to yourself, he thought. Perhaps that was an additional satisfaction to sick minds.

"How could a Bolvan insult you?" Sinkek asked.

Delvinia shook her head in disgust. "Because I have done what you warned me against a thousand times. I talked with him as a friend, once or twice, asking why he had come so far and such things. He answered, and this led to more talk."

"A dangerous pastime," Sinkek commented, but there was almost a smile on his lips and the expression on his face was becoming every moment more indulgent.

"Nor am I cured of it," Delvinia said, half laughing in self-deprecation. "Perhaps he would have kept his place had I not done what to a Bolvan is beyond forgiving. I saw another male that interested me more. Oh, I forgot," Delvinia hissed in irritation. "How should I keep all their stupid ways in mind. But this one *is* more interesting." She stepped aside to display Max fully to Sinkek and gestured toward him. "I brought my evidence with me."

Sinkek brought his full attention to Max, raking him up and down. "How?" he asked caustically.

"He is from beyond the Deadlands," Delvinia replied with triumph.

115

"Beyond the Deadlands?" Sinkek sat up and then slumped again. "Pah! A tale to beguile you." He turned his head to the Bolvi beside his chair. "It lied. Kill it!"

Before they could start for Max, Delvinia interposed her body. "No!" she exclaimed. "He did not lie. He is from beyond the lands that breed accursed ones. He is made all queer. Strip," she ordered.

Max swallowed but undid his kilt and lifted his helmet, praying that the stolen seal was well out of sight. Probably it would not have mattered. Sinkek was staring from the excrescences on Max's head to the pubic hair that partly concealed his genitals, his eyes bulging so that they looked like Delvinia's at her maddest.

"Come closer."

Wondering whether Sinkek's testing procedures would be similar to Delvinia's, Max braced himself as he obeyed. The Zel, however, did not touch him. There was a flicker of movement that caught the corner of Max's eye, but he did not dare look away from the golden orbs of the Zel. Even when a hissing whisper seemed to coil around the throne, Max continued to watch Sinkek, but the hiss seemed to recall the Zel to himself. He gestured languidly for Max to put his clothes back on, which he did hurriedly.

"Are there many people beyond the Deadlands? Many great cities?"

Max wondered whether he was hearing echoes, then realized those were the questions that had been hissed in that whisper. He risked a quick glance, but saw nothing beyond the stolid Bolvi. "Not so many people as here in the north," Max replied, "nor are the cities as fine as Salf. It may be that the curse that made the arbas fell more heavily on the southlands. We have many briski, but many die and some we must kill."

Max closed his lips tightly as if that remark was painful to make. He was anxious to discourage interest in his mythical home area without appearing unwilling to discuss it.

"You kill your briski?" Sinkek asked sharply, as if the statement had particular relevance for him.

"You see," Delvinia interrupted before Max could reply, "why I wished to keep this one? But that other fool pushed his way into my chamber and told me I was his female and that he would kill Max to make it certain. His! Can you imagine! So, of course, I stuck a knife in his throat."

Not while you were talking, Max thought. Only a Bralidom could believe a thing like that. Even a Drail could not get near enough to an armed Bolvan with a knife in hand. You got him into bed first. But Sinkek either did not realize or did not understand. He nodded indolently, then turned to the guards beside him and drawled five names.

"Seize them and kill them at evening bell—unless a mate or the eldest briska of each dies instead."

Max choked back a gasp of outrage and astonishment, but the court stood in dead and fearful silence. Plainly this was not the first time pevi had died for giving advice Sinkek did not relish. And, plainly, Sinkek was as mad as Delvinia. The only thing that was not perfectly plain was why the fearful glances of the courtiers flicked from Delvinia to Sinkek to an area Max could not see slightly behind the Zel.

Chapter 10

Max raised the pitcher to his lips and finished the last of the wine. Then he turned and looked down on Delvinia's sleeping form for a moment. He hoped he had not given her too much of the water weed, but realized, with a slight sense of shock, that he did not really care. If she lived until midnight bell, so that her servants would not raise an alarm until his duty period was finished, he would be satisfied.

The next step was a series of forgeries. First an order of release for a servant imprisoned for being drunk and disorderly. Then a letter instructing the warden of the lowest level to give what privileges Delvinia lawfully could to Zabulin. Into this he twisted several gold coins, which he filched shamelessly from the drawer. Last he copied the pass he still held, adding in the space provided at the bottom for special instructions that all should pass a prisoner released from the upper level and a guard. Last he wrote an order to bring two female larths, ripe for breeding, to a farm outside the city. To all of these he pressed Delvinia's personal seal, which he disinterred from his hair coil and then half concealed in a cluttered corner of the desk.

It had not, Max thought, been necessary to steal the seal, but he had not known he would have a chance to use Delvinia's possessions so freely. Now, if the outer guard would let him enter the dungeon levels with that pass all would be well. If general suspicion and uneasiness had been roused because of Jael's escape and the guard refused . . . Max shrugged. Either they would have to abandon Zabulin or he would have to think of another ruse. He rolled the writings and slipped them into his outer pouch and, without a backward glance, let himself out into the corridor, where he took up guard position to wait until his tour of duty was over.

When the subManili came by to check the guards, Max mentioned that Delvinia had ordered him to run an errand for her. "And I have been on duty for half a bell extra," he complained. Then he held his breath, wondering if his gambit would pay off or if the sub-Manili would offer to assign someone else to run the errand.

The officer stared at him coldly. "If Drail Delvinia has given an order, you had better obey it. You are being paid for your extra duty. If the errand is long, you may apply for more extra pay."

"I am glad to hear that," Max remarked, concealing his relief, "but what I want to know is whether I can get something to eat and drink. I have missed all meals since morning bell."

"Oh." The subManili's expression relaxed from its

disapproval. "You are finished at midnight bell? Go down to the household kitchens. They will find something for you."

Max nodded his thanks. "And will I need a pass?" he asked.

"Not for that. Be alert."

Max saluted, maintaining his indifferent expression with some trouble. Things could not be going better. He stood still, staring into space, with his brain darting here and there, putting another building block into a plan or polishing the rough edges off contingencies in others. If Max's old world had had a god, he would have knelt in thanksgiving. Never had he been so keenly alive. Nothing in that life of technological miracles had been as wonderful as the day-to-day activities of this one.

Frustrated, he offered his thanks to Yelth and Trolg, and the gesture gave him satisfaction. It was odd. In his old world Max had never felt the need of a god; here, he had to have one (or several, rather) to curse by, ask for help, and thank for favors. A wry grin twisted his lips briefly. The situation tended toward a proof of an anthropological theory that gods were a direct reflection of the state of a culture: animistic at first, then anthropomorphic, then metaphysical, and, finally, nonexistant. Recognition of this truth intellectually made no difference at all, Max realized with surprise. Emotionally he still thanked Yelth and Trolg and prayed for their further assistance with all sincerity.

Although Max had feared that time would hang heavy until his replacement came, he found enough in his thoughts to keep him busy. He exchanged passwords with the new guard and then asked which was the nearest stairway to the kitchen. He grinned appreciation as the more experienced guard gave him extremely detailed instructions and then said caustically, "I doubt if even that is sufficient for one who loses himself in the Great Halls." Max knew he would never live down that excuse, but he could afford to laugh because he knew he would be gone before the jest wore thin.

A large number of Bralidom were hard at work in the kitchen. Although hardworking Bolvi might wish to sleep after midnight, that was just about the time Bralidom nobles bent on pleasure would be wanting a snack. A pretty Bralidom female minced up to Max as soon as he entered the huge room. "And what can we do for you, Pev?" she asked, with a suggestive lift to her lips and a frank invitation in her amber eyes.

Right on the ball, Yelth, Max thought. Had a male approached him things would have been more difficult. "You can give me food," he growled, "food that I can carry with me. I have an errand to do for Drail Delvinia that cannot wait." Then, as if he really saw the female for the first time, he leered at her. "What time do you finish duty?"

"Not until morning bell," she replied, "but I can slip away . . . "

Max shook his head. "If I am slow upon the Drail's errand, I might not live to meet you again." He paused, then beckoned her a little closer. "I know a place in the garden. Pack enough food for me to eat now, and enough for us—things that will not spoil—for later. I will meet you outside"—he gestured at the door he had entered by—"at morning bell. We will have time for pleasure—and for food—and for more pleasure—"

The maid pouted a little, but she moved to do his bidding. No one conjured with Delvinia's name or delayed an instant in carrying out her orders. Max felt no compunction. This female would not have cared if his hair were white with age or he had three legs—any Bolvan would satisfy her need. In all probability she would make a connection with another Bolvan before morning bell and fail to show up at all; even if she did, she would take Max's absence as a result of his duties so that her feelings would not be hurt.

To Max's satisfaction, the maid returned with a basket she could barely carry, saying, as she thrust her burden into his arms, "I told the cook it was for a noble night party of four—no reason why we should not have the best."

Max left by the door he had entered and worked his way around to the Hall of the Seven Battles. Moonslight was strong enough, now that his eyes were accustomed to the dark, to show him most of the Hall. It was so silent, not even the faintest whisper of breath beside his own, that he stopped short. Then he stared, unbelieving, at the floor. The dust of ages lay upon it, thick and undisturbed.

Bewildered, he raised his eyes to tapestry and mural. He could not have lost himself and discovered a hitherto unvisited chamber. This *was* the Hall of the Seven Battles. And, unless he was utterly mad, this was where he had left Jael last night. Even if he had only dreamed of rescuing her, surely he had searched for her. At least his own footprints should have crossed the floor. Did he dream it all?

Again he checked the walls. Then, shaking his head, he set his basket down. He had not dreamed what happened last night because Kole had not taken him to the Hall of the Seven Battles, yet he knew its form and decorations. A chill washed over him. Maybe the whole thing was a dream and he was still in the

Consideration Chamber or the Transporter. That was nonsense. There was something wrong, but not with him. This was a trick or a trap of some kind, and the only way to find out was to spring it. Max's eyes narrowed; he bent to pick up his basket again, but took it in a special grip. It would be a shame to waste the food, but— A low gurgle of laughter, seemingly right in his ear, froze him.

"Do not step out there," Jael murmured, her voice quivering slightly with amusement. "It took me many bell-tenths to cover our trail."

She was standing just beside him, her eyes glowing faintly in the moonlight, the gleam of her teeth showing that the glossy black lips were lifted in a smile. Max was astounded. He had been listening and he had not heard her move.

"But how?"

"There were old hangings in some chambers above. First I blurred the marks, then I fanned the floor and beat the dust from the hangings. The other old hall behind I did also, but not that one with the red eyes of Trolg in it nor the front one. I made it a clear trail from where you brought me down to the unbarred door where we supposedly escaped. When the searchers came," she gurgled, "they did not even enter here. So easily were they fooled."

"You watched them?" Max asked, horrified by the chance she had taken. Then he relaxed and laughed softly. There was no sense in losing his temper about what might have happened when it had not. "Come above, where you can eat and drink more safely," he said. "I know you have questions to ask and so have I."

They settled in one of the rooms Max had not entered during the first part of his search. A number of these, not so long unused as those at the rear of the palace were still partly furnished. As Jael ate, Max told her first of his offworld origin, his adoption by her people, their plans for escape and where to meet, and then all he knew or guessed about Sinkek's plans. Finally he had a question to ask.

"So, Thal, here the path branches. Before I go further I must know your desires and what you believe our clan will desire. Sinkek must die because he has broken custom in a way that could destroy this world."

To Max's surprise, Jael looked troubled. "Customs must change," she said slowly. "Or the world will become frozen and die of its own rigidity."

For one thunderstruck moment Max stared at the beautiful female across from him. It was incredible that she could recognize so fundamental a principle instinctively. A primitive society generally resisted the concept of change even while it was changing rapidly. Impulsively he lifted her hand and kissed it. Jael did not draw away—merely cocked her head inquiringly.

"What is that?"

"A custom of my own world that expresses love and deep respect," he replied.

"Then I am honored." A gleam of interest showed in her eyes, but she took back her hand gently and Max accepted the fact that this was not the time or the place for personal affairs.

"You are right when you say customs must change. Indeed they must, but there are good ways and bad for such change. Perhaps Sinkek's central idea that all cities should be under one rule is not wrong, and it may be so in the future, but to bring that about by destroying the concept of honorable dealing between tribes—that is an abomination. If one tribe may not trust to the honor of another, this world will fall into chaos."

"I do not think it was Sinkek's idea," Jael interjected, and then, as she saw Max's expression change, she held up a hand to forestall questions. "However, he is dyed deep with evil and, if one pev must be destroyed to make a point, I can think of none Gorona would miss less than Zel Sinkek."

Setting aside a sudden deep stirring of purpose that woke when Jael intimated that Sinkek was not the initiator of the idea of unifying the cities by force, Max addressed himself to the immediate problem of what was to happen to Salf.

"That is just the point. Is it to be one pev alone, the one all tribes will associate with this evil, or will it be needful to punish the whole city of Salf?"

Jael was wide-eyed with astonishemnt. "Wherefore? What had the pevi of Salf to do with Sinkek's idiocies?"

"I do not know. Remember, I am new to this world. Among the Enthok the pevi of the clan concur with the Zeli's decisions. And, therefore, the pevi are as guilty or as innocent as the Zeli."

"Not among the Bralidom. Oh, if a Zel becomes too outrageous, the pevi of the city conspire with one or another family of nobles and they hire Bolvi secretly —or bribe the Zel's Bolvi—and the Zel and his heirs are removed. But usually the Zel rules as he wills, attending to the nobles if he attends to any at all."

"Then it seems to me that it would be best that we arrange who should be the next Zel of Salf. It would be useless to remove Sinkek and have another with the same ideas or under the same infiuence rule."

Jael's curved brow shot upward and her lips lifted into an expression of delighted cynicism. "So I think

also, but even if we set aside the minute problem of
how two fugitives are to order the succession in a clan
to which they are not related, there remains the question of how we can know who is and is not in agreement with Sinkek."

Max laughed at her way of putting the question,
but he replied soberly, explaining about Zabulin and
his supporters. Jael stared a little blankly, then her
rich chuckle bubbled out.

"I see you have a most economical nature—an asset
to any clan. Since you are here already, it would be
wasteful merely to rescue me. By all means, bring
Zabulin too. No doubt spiriting away two important
prisoners will give you no more trouble than making
one vanish."

Max grinned. "Not much more trouble, if my plan
works. What may give me trouble is making a diver-
sion so that you and Zabulin can come over the wall."

"Ah," Jael remarked with spurious gravity. "A di-
version. Some little thing to draw the guards' attention
—like starting a full-scale war?"

A delightful companion, Max thought, watching the
light dance in her silver eyes. "I had rather thought
of a medium-size fire. There is an area near the gates
that would be all the better for a cleansing with fire.
But first I must get some rope. I will need the basket,
the cloth, and the cakes."

These were quickly assembled and Max made his
way through the Halls that were in use to the usual
exit. He had a story ready, but the guard glanced in-
curiously at his burden, recognizing it as coming from
the kitchen. Unfortunately, Max had to tell his story
or the guard might want to know what he was bringing
back in the basket. He took a few steps, hesitated, and
turned back.

"There will be no trouble if I wish to return?" he asked. "There is a maid—I wish to give her—a little something I have in my quarters, and I must get it."

"I will remember you, but remain on the first level. If you are caught above, you will be in trouble." The guard laughed coarsely. "I would not waste my substance on the maids. They are willing without."

Max grimaced. "So I guessed after a few words exchanged, but I had already offered—"

The storeroom was not guarded. There were no small items of value there and transportation of bulky items past the palace gates to where they could be sold was well nigh impossible. Max wasted some time rooting around, but he knew the rope had to be there. If Sinkek was training the Bolvi to invade a city, they had to be able to scale the walls. Then he remembered that, historically speaking, cordage was kept in casks. It was only a moment longer before he found what he wanted, and he had to grin at the further evidence of how similar technological development was even in societies of widely different biological background. Convenience was convenience, whether you were a lizard or an ape.

The cordage was perfect. Max stowed his line in his basket and returned to the entrance, where the guard passed him with no more interest than a knowing leer. He met no one else in the silent Halls or corridors above and was soon stretching out in Jael's lair to sleep away the few bell-tenths that remained before he could attempt to free Zabulin.

Chapter 11

Jael woke him just before dawn. Both ate and drank sparingly. A few words confirmed their plan. Then, once again, Max went to the entrance corridor. He could hear the guards moving about and, having decided it was close enough to morning bell, he stuck his forged order for a prisoner's release into his belt. As he came out, the guard who had passed him before caught sight of the basket he was still carrying and called sharply for him to stop. Max halted at once and turned back, his face set in a scowl that was the result of tension but could be taken for rage.

"Were you not the pev who had a meeting with—"

Max spat an oath. "I am indeed. In future I will keep my mouth shut in the hearing of the Drail's servants. One heard me say I was going to eat; thus, when I got to the kitchen and found a place to— He knew just where to find me." Max pulled the forged order from his belt and thrust it into the guard's face, shaking it. As soon as he took the order and saw Delvinia's seal, he handed it back and shrugged. The Bolvan who stood before the prison exit, however, read the order.

"I do not envy you your errand," he remarked. "The warders will not be overpleased to break the usual pattern. Why not wait until morning bell?"

"Because," Max hissed, his voice thin with assumed fury, "this pretty poppet is essential to the Drail's morning service. If he is not in attendance by morning bell, the noble one says she will have the heads of the warders and mine too. And since the Drail has just had the head off Pev Reboath, I am not about to argue with her—even though she will still be asleep by morning bell. There will be plenty of wagging tongues to say if her pretty servant is late."

"Well," the guard said doubtfully, "perhaps you will be out by morning bell. If not, I will tell my replacement to expect you."

"If not," Max growled, "you had better offer prayers for me to Trolg."

The guard laughed, but was not diverted from his duty. "Leave the basket here. You cannot carry your meal down to the prison."

"It is not my meal," Max replied uncovering it. "I took a couple of bottles of wine to sweeten the warders. Is it forbidden?"

After examining the basket and its contents carefully to be sure nothing that could aid an escape was hidden, the guard shook his head. "I do not see why. There is not enough to make them drunk." He hesitated a moment longer, then said, "Leave the basket and take the bottles alone."

Halfway down the stairwell, Max paused to let the tension seep out of him. Then he replaced the order for the release of a prisoner in his pouch and took out the letter requesting privileges for Zabulin. To Max's surprise, the door of the third level was unlocked and opened by the gross jailor he had seen on his first visit. She, unfortunately, recognized him at once.

"Well, new one?" she grunted.

"Is it permitted to come in?" Max asked. "I have a message—" he hesitated artistically—"from a noble one for you."

"It is early days for you to be so trusted." She eyed him, but he stood well back, the bottles in his arms. There was no threat in his demeanor. "Take off your sword and leave it." Max obeyed and the door swung open for him to step in. He put the bottles on the table as the door was relocked and turned to face her, the twist of letter in his hand. The dull eyes flicked to the paper and then to the bottles.

"What are those?"

"A sweetener sent by the Drail."

"Uncork them."

Max laid the letter down on the table and did as he was told. A mug was thrust at him.

"Pour a third full and drink. Then from the other— a third full and drink."

Max grinned from ear to hidden ear, drinking with every sign of eagerness. "It is not often that I get to taste wine like this," he remarked appreciatively.

The jailor made no reply but picked up the letter and untwisted it. She tossed the coins idly in one hand as she read. "Sit," she croaked at Max. "The gold will pay for many torches," she remarked, then asked, "Do you know what the letter says?"

"I do not inquire into the Drail's affairs," Max replied dryly. "I am not that new. But I suppose she desires favors for someone. And, I suppose, the gold is more for you than for torches."

The ugly gargling laugh rose, shaking the obese flesh. "What would I do with gold? I am condemned, as much as those within, except for the power I have, and light, and what dainties I desire. You feel well?" she questioned sharply.

"Indeed I do." Max wondered for what crime she had been thrust forever into the dark and how she could find that fate preferable to death, but all the while he kept his eyes fixed on the bottles. "If you have as much of such things as you desire," he said hesitantly, "perhaps you would not mind if I took another drink? Perhaps I could take a bottle with me?"

The choking gargle sounded again. "No, you cannot take the bottles, but I will have a drink with you. They are not so generous with wine. A drunken warder is no desirable thing—as the Drail doubtless knows. But she is a fool if she thinks I will not report this. There is no way to buy me!"

She poured for herself and for Max and they drank.

"It is nothing to me," Max replied, "but from what I have seen today, it is not safe to report evil of Drail Delvinia." He went on to tell the warden of what had happened and she listened avidly, absently reaching for the bottle and refilling the mugs again as the tale of the escaped Enthok, the dead Bolvan guard, and the condemned nobles unfolded. Then Max had to display his peculiarities yet again and while she marveled— and Max wondered whether it would not be simpler just to stay naked—she had still more wine and pressed more on him. Max wondered uneasily how much more wine he could hold. A far smaller amount of water weed had had a far greater effect on Delvinia.

At last, however, he noticed that the dull eyes were

even duller and the tiny head was sinking into the folds of flesh that obscured the neck and chin. Suddenly she interrupted Max in the middle of a sentence.

"You must go." The voice came through bubbles of phlegm and the words were slurred.

There was as yet no suspicion. The obese warden probably thought she had had too much wine. He contrived to look offended. "At least let me finish my drink, since you have already poured it for me." Max lifted the cup to his mouth, then set it down and started to push back his chair as the obese female struggled to rise. "All right, all right," he said sullenly, "I will go, but you know I am new to this place. I do not know all the ins and outs of fine manners. I am sorry if I offended you."

He backed away as the creature muzzily fumbled for her weapons, knowing that something was wrong. Her total loyalty to a loathsome duty was puzzling to Max, but he was very happy to realize that she was not relieved by other jailors. The traffic on the lowest level was not heavy so that while the warden slept there was little chance that Zabulin's escape would be discovered.

Although it was now apparent that the jailor was incapable of following him, Max waited until she collapsed totally before he took her keys and opened the door to the cell area. The blackness and silence were absolute, not even broken by the whimpers Max had heard on his first visit .He counted cells, then called softly, "Zabulin." No reply. Max cursed softly. If the Drail had been moved or killed, he had gone to a lot of trouble for nothing. "Zabulin," he called louder.

"Who is that?"

"He who threw you money. Now I have come to take you out of here." Max unlocked the door and drew the stunned young Drail out. Then he opened the cell of the dying prisoner. Something was still there —dead or alive Max did not stop to discover. Max removed it, humped the thin coverings on the empty pallet so that something appeared to be there, and deposited the poor creature in Zabulin's cell. All this while Zabulin stood like a paralytic, unable to believe his eyes. Max looked him over quickly. Fortunately, his luxurious cloth kilt had long since been given to the jailor to sell for torch money. He was clad in little more than a leather rag. Max led him back to the main chamber, where he mixed the remainder of the wine with dirt and dust and began to work it liberally into Zabulin's hair and skin. These, already matted and covered with filth, turned a dirty brown with the addition of the wine.

The young Drail had been so stunned by the sudden reversal of his fate that he had been totally passive. Finally, he stammered, "But what—what are you doing?"

"*We* are escaping," Max said, grinning. "Your name is—quick, does Delvinia have a young male servant about your size and age?"

"My size? My age? Delvinia! *Delvinia* is contriving my escape?" He drew back a little, as if the prison he had left would be a safe haven compared to falling into Delvinia's hands.

"No, no," Max soothed. "She is asleep like the jailor and knows nothing about it. I used her seal to forge an order of release for a servant of hers drunk and disorderly in the town. So pick a name for yourself in case the guard asks—but be sure it is not a pev the guard would know."

Swallowing hard, Zabulin shook his head. "I do not think it will be possible. You see I—I love swordplay and I have spent much time with the Bolvi. Many know me well—well enough to recognize me even under all this dirt."

Max paused a moment, then said grimly, "In two bell-thousandths I can make your face so that your own mother would not recognize it—but it will hurt."

The large gold eyes gazed pleadingly at Max. "Will I be very ugly?" he whispered.

"For a few days kind-hearted pevi will look elsewhere," Max replied with a grin, and then, impatiently, "No one you know will see you for a time. It does not take long for a black eye, a swollen nose and lips to heal."

"Oh!" Zabulin's eyes lit. "You will beat me so that I appear to have been in a fight." He laughed softly. "Forgive me. My brain is dull from going over and over the same things. I thought you would cut off my nose or scar me. Do it then. Quickly."

Zabulin started to close his eyes and brace himself, but before his fists could clench, Max hit him four times and caught him before the force of the blows could knock him down. Blood poured from nose and lips and a cut below the eye and on the opposite side on the jawline opened and began to ooze. Zabulin gasped and tried to steady himself for another onslaught.

"Finish," he urged, his voice shaking.

"I am finished," Max assured him. "Let us just be sure your hide is dirty enough while that eye and cheek swell up properly."

"But it did not hurt," Zabulin protested dazedly.

"It will," Max said dryly as he smeared blood from the streaming nose liberally over Zabulin's forehead, cheeks, forearms, and knuckles. Finally Max drew his knife and handed it to the young Drail. "Here, press the flat of the blade to the sides of your nose and to the back of your neck. I must clean up this mess and clean myself off too. When we come to the guards, keep your head down, as if you are still dazed or ashamed."

By the time Max was ready, Zabulin was no longer complaining that his bruises did not hurt. His nose had stopped bleeding and his eye and lips were nicely swelled. It was unfortunate that the eye was not discolored, but the dried blood very nearly concealed that. He examined Zabulin one last time, but could see only a slender, drooping, much befouled Bralidom nothing like the exquisite, bejeweled courtiers. The room where the warden still snorted and gurgled in her doped sleep carried no trace of their activities. The wine bottles stood empty on the table, the mugs, one empty, one half full, were positioned much as Max remembered them. Perhaps the dazed jailor would believe that Max had left when he appeared to. In any case he had done what he could to muddy the trail.

At the top of the stairs, Max took the release order and his pass from his pouch again. "Weep," he whispered to Zabulin. "Put your hands to your face to hide your shame." Then he rapped sharply with his dagger hilt. The prompt grating sound of the bar being lifted was music to his ears. It indicated strongly that no suspicion of his purpose had unsettled the guard.

As soon as the door was open, Max thrust the papers into the guard's hand. The Bolvan looked from the trembling form and half-averted face of Zabulin to the blood-spattered, filthy kilt. His lip lifted, half in derision, half in sympathy. Max danced from one foot to the other with impatience.

"By Yelth's mercy, check our passes and let us go.

Drail Delvinia will hang us both by our private parts. I was supposed to have this one—" Max gestured disgustedly with his head—"ready for duty at morning bell—and that time is already past."

The guard laughed, but he handed back the papers without even looking at them. "Kuth said you would be coming out with a thorn in your tail. Go. I would not keep you from your pleasure."

"Oh, that. This one—" Max looked daggers at his shuddering companion—"has already robbed me of that. All I hope now is to avoid punishment. Come." Max put a hand on Zabulin's back and shoved so hard that the young Drail sprawled forward onto the floor, letting out a whimper of pain.

"Go, go," the other guard agreed, waving away the pass.

Zabulin struggled halfway up and Max grasped the ragged cord belt that held his kilt, hurrying him through the doors in a bent-over position that totally obscured his features. He continued the bum's-rush technique until they had passed through into the Hall of the Red Larth. Here he moved hurriedly behind a tapestry, as if to go upstairs.

"But you have brought me inside the palace," Zabulin mumbled fearfully through his swollen lips. "You have trapped me. You fool! They will kill us both. Sinkek could not kill me outright because I have friends and there is enough unrest. Now he can say, truthfully, I was found escaping."

Max laughed. "But you will not be found. Neither friend nor enemy contrived your escape. Clan Vinci of the Enthok contrived it because, being pevi, they wish no ill to Salf. Sinkek has offended them—worse, has broken custom—and Sinkek must pay, but Salf must have a Zel. If your friends will be true, you may be that Zel."

Fear still looked out of the golden eyes, but subtly it had changed. "Sinkek—Sinkek is only a tool. Bithe must pay."

Chapter 12

Max did his best to suppress a rising feeling of exultation. Overconfidence could still breed a mistake that would bring disaster, but, sheltered in a grove of trees that acted as a windbreak between the fields, it was hard to remember they were not yet safe. The escape had gone so smoothly: the fire Max had set had burned merrily enough to draw all attention; Jael and Zabulin had come over the wall without being noticed; they had passed the open fields without pursuit. Now evening was drawing on and, as soon as it was dark, they could steal whatever they needed from the nearest farm and be on their way.

Zabulin, utterly drained, lay asleep. Jael was making friends with her new larth. She reached for a tidbit from the basket and held it out. The little clawed forepaws grasped eagerly and the beast nudged her with its ugly snout. Beulah, jealous, scratched at Max, and he gave her a selin leg. Turning, he saw that Jael's eyes rested speculatively on the sleeping Drail.

"You do not trust him?" Max asked softly.

"I trust him so far as believing he will not run back to Sinkek. I think he is earnest enough in his hatred for Bithe——"

"Who is this Bithe?" Max interrupted.

"That," Jael replied with lifted brows, "is a very, very good question." Her tone was light, but behind her eyes was something Max did not like.

"I have seen it—which is more than almost anyone else can say."

"What is it? Bolvan? Ehthok? Bralidom?"

Jael shook her head. "I said that wrong. I have seen its outer garments. I believe that is all anyone—even Sinkek—has ever seen."

"What did it say to you?"

"Nothing."

"Nothing?"

"It came one time with Sinkek to—I think to look me over as one judges a breeding larth."

"Then you think it was Bithe who wished to see what a mixture of Enthok and Bralidom would make?"

"I do not really know what to think. If so, it is the only one on Gorona who does not know that such mixtures are as good—sometimes even better—than the parents. Our ways of life usually divide us, but some always desire other ways. There has been crossing enough."

Max's sense of purpose rose like a tide of warmth in him. "An offworlder!" he exclaimed.

Jael was staring at him with a slightly startled hope in her eyes. "I wish that were true. I wish——"

"You wish that were true!" Max protested. "You do not know what you are saying. I came naked and alone from my world, because my world does not desire to conquer or even to trade with other worlds. But my world and others have weapons that could turn a city like Salf into dust, could burn the whole of Gorona to ash, could crack this planet open and let its heart run out into space."

Instead of displaying horror or disbelief, Jael merely nodded. "I have no doubt it is so." And in reply to Max's obvious amazement, she continued, "You have not seen our arbas. There is one where half the city has been melted into glass—smooth. There are huge lakes where arbas once were. We know, because we can see the shattered buildings lying under the water, and the water is so clear because nothing lives in it and it is death to drink. Nothing grows on the shores, and further back the plants are strange."

"If you know this," Max muttered aghast, "you know such weapons cannot be fought with swords."

"Assuredly. But I ask you, why should offworlders turn such weapons against us? If Bithe is an offworlder, why slink in muffling garments and whisper in Sinkek's ear? If there is something on Gorona his world wants, why not ask or even demand? Why urge Sinkek to swallow Degat? Surely it would be to the advantage of offworlders to keep the cities apart."

She made disgustingly good sense, which for some reason made Max more uncomfortable. "If offworlders with such weapons are a pleasant relief to you, what in the names of Yelth and Trolg do you fear?" he hissed irritably.

Jael's eyes were suddenly silver pools of desolation. "The Old Ones."

Max gaped. "But they are dead! Ages dead!"

"We hope. We pray." Jael's hands clasped in a very human gesture of supplication before her breast. "But who painted that scene in the Hall of the Red Eyes of Trolg? What pev hung in the sky to see Gorona as a huge ball below him? Only the Old Ones could do that."

She was trembling. Jael, who had never once shown a sign of fear. Max took the clasped hands in his. "Jael, I assure you they can have no weapons more terrible than those of offworlders, and no more reason to use them. If you do not fear offworlders, why fear the Old Ones?"

"They made us," she cried softly. "We are their creatures! We must obey them."

And suddenly part of the dream Max had had the first night he had been on Gorona came back. One man alone was not to change a world or keep it from changing. The world would grow in its own way—if it could be freed from its incubus. Gently Max drew Jael toward him, turning so that he could slip an arm around her.

"But if this is true, why be secret? Bithe has only to stand up and order the cities to obey. If the pevi *must* obey, what has it to fear?"

"Other Old Ones." She turned her face up to his, a frown wrinkling over her brow ridges. "Every pev knows—ah, I keep forgetting, even when we speak of it, that you are not of our people. You do not know!"

"I have heard a scrap here and there about the Old Ones, but between one thing and another there was no time for a history course."

Jael relaxed a little more into his arms and closed her eyes. "In the old songs and scrolls the nampu keep, the tale runs thus. When the red eyes of Trolg were suns, and the green sun was only a brightness in the sky, the Old Ones came here from the world that hangs between the red eyes."

"Jael," Max protested, "you are talking about ten times hundreds of millions of years."

Her teeth flashed. "We did not write this part. We have copied from the writings of the Old Ones. If we existed at all, it was as worms in the sea."

Max did not answer that. He could not get his mouth closed. What Jael was telling him might be real history. A totally nontechnological people does not glibly accept space travel and understand evolution at the same time that it does not know how to make fire from twirling sticks or rocks. That is a memory no people who have it ever forget completely. Thus the early history of the pevi was in a technological society where there was no need ever to "make" fire and where their ancestors were in contact with space travel and had been taught about evolution.

"They came not long before the Great Chaos, thinking they would be far enough away to be safe—"

"The Great Chaos?"

"That was the time when the red eyes of Trolg were born out of the blue suns. While those ate themselves up, the green mist grew together and became much brighter. By the time the red eyes of Trolg were as they are now and the green sun shone steadily, the Old Ones were many and their skills were great. Life was rich and easy for them. They sought new things and games to play to fill their time." Her voice faltered and then she said, defiantly, "We are the outcome of one of their games."

There were advantages and disadvantages, Max thought, to knowing without doubt that you were not the special creation of Almighty Heaven. It saved you from the Inquisition and saddled you with a Master Race. "I do not see that there is any difference between being a result of the game of the Old Ones and the result of an accident of blind chance, as I am. If I had a choice, I think I would choose your beginnings over my own."

The silver eyes, which had been downcast, flew to his face.

"You do not even have to tell me the rest of the story," Max continued. "I know it because the fruiting is buried in the seed. Three groups of Old Ones engaged in breeding experiments and produced the Bolvi, the Bralidom, and the Enthok, each for a different purpose. Meanwhile, other Old Ones were playing less harmless games. They produced the weapons to make the war that made the arbas."

"Yes, you are right."

"But what I cannot guess is what happened to them. The pevi survived. Some arbas were destroyed, but from what I have heard many stand intact except for the wearing away of time."

The trouble deepened on Jael's face. "This is the time of the incomplete scrolls. We know that some weapons were of sickness, and that sickness did not touch the pevi. Other weapons burned and destroyed the arbas, but we do not think the pevi lived in the arbas. The records of the Old Ones falter into silence, and the pevi, then, did not write scrolls. I do not think the pevi were the same as we are now."

"I am sure you were not. Probably you were very little more than beasts, only in you a—a seed for a brain that would grow bigger and bigger had been planted by the Old Ones. The growth and the flowering were your own—as will be the fruiting still to come."

Jael was silent for a moment as the full weight of that idea sank into her, but she did not comment on the remark. "Of the years that followed we have no records, only legends. Lacking more, the scrolls used the legends. These say that a few Old Ones survived. Some enslaved us; some raised us and taught us as children; most withdrew to some secret fastness. Then those who loved us rose up and destroyed those who enslaved us. And then there are no more mentions of Old Ones, even in the legends. They do not say they all died. There lies our fear. If they have lived all these years in some secret place and now have chosen to return, we are still their creatures—"

"You are not!" Max said indignantly. "You were never their creatures after you had begun to think for yourselves. Are your briski your 'creatures'? Yet you made them, more surely than any Old One made you. Do your briski obey you without argument?"

Jael laughed. "Only when I am close enough to land a blow."

"And you, I believe, are a wise Thal. But I cannot see any reason at all to be obedient to a bunch of idiots that destroyed themselves and nearly destroyed their world. I am sorry if I offend you, but despite their powerful weapons and their 'skills' that is what your Old Ones were—a bunch of idiots!"

The silver eyes stared, reproach and shock warring with anger. No one likes to learn that his god has feet of clay. At last a tiny little sound, like the beginning of a whimper, forced itself through her lips; her shoulders shook. Max tightened his grip upon her, seeking words of comfort—until he realized she was laughing. "So be it. As long as no Old One is close enough to land a blow—I will do as I please."

"That is not good enough, Jael." Max said quietly. "Old One or offworlder, Bithe is close enough. It has already landed a blow upon Clan Vinci by leading

Sinkek to break custom. Will you swallow this, permitting it to change—"

"But there is the problem," Jael interrupted. The fear was gone from her face, but it was very troubled and intent. "I am not sure Bithe's idea is wrong. In a certain way it will work hardship upon the Enthok, for to unite the cities will mean the end of our profit in fighting, but is that fighting a good—"

"Nor am I sure the idea is wrong," Max cut in. "But Bithe's *way* is wrong. We have spoken of that before. An end to fighting must grow of itself, other things growing at the same time. It cannot be forced ahead of its time by breaking custom."

Jael nodded uncertainly and then, after a pause, with more determination. "Yes, even if Bithe is an Old One. It is still the wrong way and, I think with you, the wrong time. That is my judgment, heart and mind, and I must follow that guide now as I have all my life before."

"Besides," Max suggested, "we do not *know* Bithe is an Old One. Perhaps it is an offworlder, like myself, who can look for no help from its people—perhaps an escaped criminal—and cannot return. Perhaps it wished to carve out a kingdom for itself—"

"And who should know one offworlder better than another offworlder," Jael responded with cynical conviction. "You are right. From now on, Bithe is an offworlder—even if it must be an offworlder pretending to be an Old One. That is our tale. We are sure of it."

Chapter 13

A silver ghost flitted silently out of the low brush growing along the cliff face, straightened up, and resolved itself into Jael. Max was pleased that he had guessed right about where to watch for her. He was growing self-conscious about his clumsiness in woodcraft.

"Luck cannot hold forever," she breathed softly. "The trackers have picked up our trail."

"How many?" Rather than being disappointed, Max was almost relieved. He had begun to fear that there were trackers that Jael had not spotted and that they would lead them right to the Enthok encampment.

"Too many," Jael replied grimly. "There are eight at least, with at least two larths to a man as well as pack animals. We cannot outrun them."

Zabulin's breath hissed in audibly, but he did not speak.

"I never intended that." Max rose and turned to

riding. He felt a twinge of anticipatory sympathy for the Bolvi. Softly Max drew alongside his guide. She pointed left, held up three fingers, fisted her hand and opened it twice. Then she pointed straight ahead. An open hand—five—and three fists opened wide—times fifteen—seventy-five. Max nodded gently; he had learned that any body movement shifted weight, and shifting weight often produced unexpected sound. Jael slid away to the right and disappeared in the shadows.

Max sighted on a pale tree trunk he thought far enough away. Thirty paces. Keeping his eye on his pale marker, he turned until his shoulder lined up on it. He sighted ahead again. At fifty paces Max stopped and listened; nothing but the wind. That did not mean others could not hear him, only that he could not hear. At sixty he did not need to stop. A larth's startled hiss sounded ahead and to the right. With all his strength, Max flung the large rock he had been carrying for some time toward the camp but to the left, flung another, uttered a loud groan, and began to run swiftly and noisily toward the camp.

The bait was not cast in vain. A hubbub of voices arose, giving Max direction and covering the sounds he was now trying not to make. When he could see movement, he uttered another loud groan, then veered off to the left again. He went a little slower now, more intent on keeping his noise down than on making speed. He did not wish to go all around the camp and come up behind Jael. A sharp crackle stopped him in his tracks. Horrified, he watched the ground belch angry smoke while a small bush in the area he had just left flamed briefly and crumpled into ash.

Max clenched his teeth over an unuttered cry of rage and warning. It was fortunate his body was trained to react without thought because his brain was paralyzed. Somehow he was belly flat, inching forward, the skin on his back rippling, the hairs rising in terrified expectation of being broiled. An energy weapon on Gorona! The enormity of the idea at first blanked out all but trained physical response. Then thought returned, but it brought only questions. Would Bithe trust an energy weapon to a Bolvan? How many would it have dared to bring? Was it the only whatever-it-was or was this blaster wielder another one? And then, overriding all questions, an answer of sorts. This hunt was not for Jael. One does not fire a blaster at a fugitive whose only value is as a hostage.

A low ridge of blackness ahead. Max inched cautiously, for him, silently. A trace of moisture had returned to his fear-dried mouth when his hand touched stone rather than dead wood. A boulder. He circled behind it, low as possible, drew a deep, trembling breath, and tossed a tiny pebble away to the right behind him and, a moment later, to the left. Head down, arms curled over it, Max offered up a single silent prayer. But there was no wash of heat, no crackle of flame. Had that single bolt been a surprise-born mistake?

The whole camp was awake now. Max could hear the pevi talking but could not understand. He could even see a few in outline, and they certainly were not robed and cowled. Moonslight glittered briefly as pevi tightened harness. They must be Bolvi. Another hiss came from the tethered larths. Max swallowed. Even if Jael had noticed that flash of fire, she would not know what it meant. Max had a vivid image of Jael's silk-soft gleaming silver a crackling, carbonized ruin. In a single movement he was up on the rock. A second leap carried him to within bars of the Bolvi so swiftly that they were still turning when he landed in a crouch and was up, weaving, checking, leaping, and crouching in a memory-ingrained pattern that needed no thought. A crackle, a belch of smoke, but it was where he should have been, not where his erratic pattern had placed him.

Long leap, short run, stop dead, whirl. A knife-edge blow felled one of the Bolvi, who were shouting and bumping into each other in a mad effort to guess where Max would land next. Another crackle. Damn! Max hadn't even seen the smoke that time. To stop to look was death, but to be unable to discover the position of the blaster wielder was death also. How many charges did such a weapon carry?

Crouch, slow step, half turn, leap. Max's eyes swept the tethered larths. They seemed to be moving uneasily. Jael? The blaster wielder?

Straight jump, run back, whirl, sidestep, crouch. Another Bolvan came within reach and went down. Then two converged, one from each side. A high kick ended one threat, a low block and pharynx blow finished the other.

Whirl, leap right, whirl, leap right, short step, full turn. A sword gleaming. Max ducked, kicked, side-stepped, leaped straight up, did a rear back spring. A crackle. Max gasped an oath that was drowned in the screams of the Bolvan caught by the blast. One thing he was sure of. This bolt had been fired from a different position than the last. So the blaster wielder was moving—or there was more than one.

Run back, half turn, leap back, leap right, step forward, half turn. It was not only fear that was making Max's breath come in short gasps now. He was tiring. Yet surely he had performed antiweapons maneuvers in competitions at home for longer periods without fatigue. It made a difference, Max thought wryly, whether a friendly foe was trying to mark you with a squirt of colored ink or a real enemy was trying to fry you.

Whirl, whirl. Suddenly Max gasped another oath. The larths were gone! One moment all of them were there, the next they were not.

Crouch down, leap right, stop dead, run right—and keep running. The dash for the cover of the trees was, he hoped, as unexpected as everything else. In any event, no flick of flame touched him beyond the burning of his lungs and the searing pangs of cramps in legs and abdomen. Max ignored the pain. He had been trained for that and it was easy. Run! Run! Where was Jael? Which direction was camp? Never mind that! Run!

There are signals in the body that tell the trained athlete when further exertion will go beyond the pain of stress and blank the mind or stop the heart. On signal, Max made one long desperate leap sideways and back from the straight line of his run and dropped to the ground. His last effort was to roll over twice, hoping earth and leaves would stick to his sweat-wet skin and offer a bit of camouflage. Then there was mind and strength for nothing but the fight against screaming in agony as his cells struggled to restore the chemical balance of his body. When you cannot get enough oxygen to burn the fuel needed for extra exertion, you can borrow against future breathing and use anaerobic respiration. Money or oxygen, the borrowing is not so bad, but paying back is plain hell.

Finally, trembling like a quivering aspen, Max found strength enough to crawl into a thicket. Thus far there was no sign of pursuit, which was not too surprising. Unless Jael had been off in her scouting, there were only two Bolvi left and the whatever-it-was. The five Max had felled would be in no condition to pursue anything, especially on foot, for a while, and the sixth —Max hoped for his sake that he was dead. Probably those capable of pursuit had followed the clear trail of the larths, but Jael would be in no danger for a while, for she was riding. Max could afford to rest a little longer.

The blaster was not meant for Jael. In fact, she was a greater danger dead than alive. Besides, there was no reason for the trackers to believe she was in the group. It was Zabulin they were pursuing. He was a threat both to Sinkek and Bithe. Zabulin had not been executed out of hand only because he had strong supporters in Salf, but he had escaped. If he were brought back to Salf dead—not by sword or spear but by some inexplicable cause like burning—the blame could not fall on Sinkek and the threat would be removed.

Energy renewed by a new sense of urgency, Max slid from his thicket and began to jog steadily. As soon as the trees thinned a little he could see the red eyes of Trolg and had his direction. Although he tried to be quiet, speed was now more essential than silence, and he made good time down the fault. An odd-shaped rock formation brought him nearly to a stop. He was not far from the campsite now. Softly he moved right, cursing under his breath as twigs cracked when he passed through the brush at the cliff face. A step brought more crackling. How Jael moved over the same ground without a sound remained a mystery. Max bent into a crouch that would make him about the same size and shape as a gobari and gave up any attempt at silence. He moved forward, paused as if to graze, moved forward again. With luck the sounds, completely incautious as they were, would be attributed to a feeding animal.

The campfire showed a dull red glow which was re-inforced only by the dim, lurid light of the red eyes of Trolg. The green moons had set, It was very quiet. Max moved a step or two, like an animal, cautious, but drawn by the fire. His heart leaped into his mouth. The larths were gone, all of them, and an errant breeze suddenly brought the stench of burned flesh. Max's involuntary movement rusted leaves where no gobari could reach.

"Down!" Jael's voice rang clear. "Have a care!"

Simultaneously two forms rose from concealment and Max leaped forward. Flame blossomed close enough to make him gasp with pain. He leaped sideways, but this was no spot for maneuvering. Brush caught his ankle and he fell. Death! He nearly screamed with terror, but his throat was too dry to emit a sound. Reflex brought him up, running to the attack although it was hopeless. He was too far away to strike before the blaster could be reactivated.

He had dodged a sword blade and struck down the wielder before it occurred to him that he should not even have had time to worry about dying. The second blast should have caught him as he fell or, at the latest, as he lay on the ground. But the mind had not caught up with the body. Max was whirling, looking for the second opponent, when he saw Jael. Lips drawn thin with hatred, she was pulling the knife she had thrown out of the blaster wielder. Blade in hand she knelt beside her victim.

"Where had you this burner?" she hissed.

"Bithe," the Bolvan sighed.

"Have you carried it all the way?"

"Yes."

"And you used it in the camp?"

"Yes."

"Has Bithe other such?"

"How could I know?"

For a moment Jael stared, her eyes black fathomless pools in her face, which, under the red eyes of Trolg, looked bloody. Then, quite casually, she brought the knife down in a sweeping arc, right through the Bolvan's temple.

Max uttered a choked cry, half protest, half recognition. Jael! Now he knew why the name had been so familiar. Jael and Sisera. Jael had killed Sisera, the enemy of her people, by hammering a nail into his head. Max remembered laughing about it once, saying that it was silly. No one would just lie still while a nail was hammered into his head. But a strong arm and a sharp point . . . Max shuddered.

"Why did you kill him?" he whispered.

The bloody mask with its hollowed eyes lifted to him. "As a warning. That one—" she gestured toward the Bolvan who lay unconscious from Max's blow— "will bring the word that one of us slew a man already wounded. The Bolví know the Enthok do not do such. They know you do not kill. They will understand that these things—" her head jerked slightly toward the blaster—"are anathema. Who touches them is accursed. Who uses them—dies."

Max expected to feel horror and revulsion—what he did feel was approval. He was not even sorry for the Bolvan. Every pev knew the arbas and the tale of the Old Ones. No pev should be willing to use an energy weapon. Well, perhaps he was a little sorry. If the Bolvan had obeyed Bithe as an Old One . . . A wash of rage passed over Max against Bithe, whatever it was. Offworlder or Old One, Bithe certainly knew better.

It was not that Max believed Gorona to be a Garden of Eden. The pevi were too "human" to live in Paradise. Perhaps they were just as stupid as "knowing man" and would burn up their own world. If so, it was their affair—to conceive of the weapons, invent them, build them, and use them. His purpose was clear and he acknowledged the wisdom of it. No whatever-it-was would set the pevi down at the end of that path of destruction when they had not yet even started along it. Perhaps this society, so different in some ways from the primitive situation on his own world, could work out its problems without a second atomic disaster. In any case, Max would try to give it its chance. He took a shaky step forward and held out his hand to Jael.

The black pools glinted up at him. His body blocked the light of the fire and the red eyes of Trolg so that her dear, familiar silver face turned to him. "I saw," she murmured caressingly. "I saw you dance with death in that camp." She rose smoothly and stepped over the Bolvan's corpse, coming so close that breast and thigh touched Max. "I have never seen such a wonder in my life. I am Thal of my people and a free female. Are you willing to share tent and bed with me?"

"I have no tent and no bed in this world beyond what your people have lent me, but I will share anything that is mine—my body, my life."

"It is more than sufficient."

Max bent his head to fasten his mouth to the ebony lips. He had barely touched them, however, when the tainted breeze washed over them. His grip on Jael tightened convulsively. It might have been her. "Beloved," he murmured, "I would rather kiss you, but I suppose we had better bury Zabulin."

Jael stiffened in his arms. "Bury him? Oh, Max, even

if his treachery brought this upon us—and I do not really believe it it so—should we not kill him first? To bury him alive—"

"You mean that isn't Zabulin I smell?" Max interrupted. Then, half laughing, he explained his reasoning about the blaster.

"No," Jael said, "if that was the purpose, it has failed. Zabulin is safe. As soon as I returned, we hid ourselves well because I knew they would follow the larths. It was a larth the fool struck. The poor silly creature." Her voice trembled with rage. "If I had time I would have killed that filth by cebars. To hurt a larth —no one would hurt a larth."

"It was not done by intention," Max soothed. "He was not, I am sure, accustomed to the weapon. Bithe told him only to point it and push the firing stud, I would guess. He saw something move—that was all. It was why I came alive out of that camp too."

"No," Jael objected, lifting her head proudly. "That was your skill—I saw."

Max was not nearly as convinced as she was, but considering the effect that what she believed had on her, he made no further disclaimer. Instead he turned his head toward the weapon. "We cannot leave that thing here to be returned to Bithe, and I do not know how to destroy it."

Jael hunched her slim shoulders with distaste. "We must take it with us. We can drop it in a river or—no, perhaps we should show it to Xers and Ptar. If Bithe has others and arms the Bolvi with them, the clan must know what it faces." She glanced at Max with pride. "I do not think you can teach them your magic in time."

"No," Max agreed, but absently. "We had better

get downwind of the odor of burned larth. Perhaps if she cannot smell it, Beulah will come to my whistle. If she does not come, we are little better off than the Bolvi."

Chapter 14

Beulah returned readily to Max's whistle, bringing with her the other larths, trembling and hissing with fright but eager to follow any leader. The extra animals were a manifold benefit, providing relief mounts and mounts for hunting as well. Although Jael had never been in this part of the country before, she had little trouble heading them in the right direction, and finally they came to an area she recognized because she had hunted in it when they had visited the arbas in the past.

Before they went down into the open river valley, Jael scouted ahead to determine how far south of the arbas her people were encamped. She returned somewhat troubled because another clan of Enthok, considerably larger than her own, was encamped on the river. The tents of Clan Vinci she did not see at all.

"Is there some reason to fear a strange clan?" Max asked.

"Fear? Oh, no, but I am worried about my people."

"The quicker down, the quicker we will have answers."

They were hardly out onto the plain when their easy decision seemed a mistake. A troop boiled from between the tents riding larths goaded to their best speed. Jael stopped, doubt filling her silver eyes. "I do not like—" she began.

A long-drawn, ululating cry drifted up the valley— a peculiar fluting call that could be heard, Max guessed, for many bibars. He tensed, ready to turn Beulah to run or dismount and fight—whichever Jael thought better. Instead of either, she startled him by whipping her larth forward.

"Xers!" she shrieked. "Xers!"

The next bell-tenth was one of wild confusion. Max would not have believed a people so calm in defeat could become so hysterical with joy. He was kissed and embraced, carried and carressed. Even Beulah was kissed. It was highly embarrassing, as Max had no previous experience with a hero's welcome. All of his past exploits had been received with—to say the least —less enthusiasm. And no sooner had the excitement begun to abate when the leaders of the other clan arrived and the celebration, although on a slightly more restrained note, began all over again.

When calm had finally been restored and they had returned to the encampment, Ptar said, "Come to my tent. I had forgotten in my joy to give orders that your tents be set up." And Jael cast a look of admonition at Max. It was necessary, right now, to make a public statement of their relationship, but he had not the faintest notion of the proper form.

"I am of this clan by your generosity," he began hesitantly.

160

"You are of this clan by acts greater than we can repay," Ptar stated positively. "What is ours to the last drop of blood or splinter of silver or steel is yours for the asking."

Max smiled and shook his head. "You owe me nothing. However, I am still a stranger in some ways, and I fear to offend or break some custom of which I am ignorant, for what I wish to ask is a very great thing."

"We are not fools to take offense at ignorance," Xers exclaimed.

"No, but this is so very—I wish to bind myself more firmly to you. I desire a mate of your people."

Both Xers and Ptar looked utterly dumbfounded. "But I do not understand," Ptar began, and a troubled frown creased the younger Zel's brow. "We offered you anything," Xers added, "but if the female is unwilling—"

Jael hissed with irritation. "She is not unwilling. I am the female."

There was an instant of silence followed by a roar of laughter. "Pev Max," Xers chortled, "that is the third miracle—that I know of—that you have wrought. But if Jael is willing, it is nothing to do with us. She has bred four briski of four different fathers—as is the Thal's duty—and she is free to take any male to mate that she desires. You could have told him," he added disapprovingly to Jael.

She raised indignant brows. "How should I know he had such doubts? His people must have been very strange. I thought he was troubled because he came naked and without possessions. I thought he would ask for a tent and furnishings—a fair reward."

"But the captured larths are worth—Twenty larths are a rich pev's herd," Ptar assured Max.

"They are Jael's," Max remarked. "She took—"

He was interrupted by a violent hiss, half laughing, half exasperated from Jael, who came and took his arm possessively. "I thought to save the clan expense, knowing he would ask less than you desired to give —but he is hopeless. Let provision be made equivalent to his worth to the clan. Now," she said to Max, "you will see the result of overgreat modesty."

Morning brought a full war council of both clans. First Ptar summed up what had happened since Max left, describing their accidental meeting with Clan Sivio, who had been Degat's mercenaries, the explanations, and the decision of Sivio's Zeli to join Clan Vinci in bringing Sinkek to justice. Then Jael described her experiences and Max's rescue. When she reseated herself cross-legged on the hides serving for seats, all eyes turned to Max.

He rose and looked out over the angry and determined faces. He had a strong impulse to beg them to spare Salf, to speak of the long-range benefits of mercy and moderation, but he swallowed it down. This was a new world and it must learn its own lessons; its culture must develop in its own way. Max spoke of purely practical matters—the training the Bolvi had received, what he knew of the way the gates were guarded, and last of the open door into Sinkek's palace up over the wall and through the deserted area from which Jael had escaped.

Tarbe of Clan Sivio saw the difficulty with that path at once. "For two to come down it would not be hard, but for the pevi of two clans the road is too narrow."

"The road might be broadened somewhat with ladders," Max said.

"Not enough to fight the number of Bolvi Sinkek has," Ptar judged. "In a confined space where the ability to charge and retreat as a unit is lost, the Bolvi and the Enthok are not unevenly matched. Clan Vinci is very willing to die so that no other pevi should break custom as Sinkek has, but we must get to Sinkek before we die."

Max agreed with that sentiment heartily. "But," he pointed out, "if an assault were launched at one or two gates at almost the same time, before the wall climbers were discovered, many more might mount before discovery, and few Bolvi would be free to attack them."

The five Zeli stared. (Sivio had three, one only a few years older than Rib, Jael's eldest briska.) Then Tarbe smiled slowly and looked at Ptar. "Will you share this stranger of yours with us Ptar, as you have shared the secret of the firestones he showed you?"

"He is not for sharing," Jael laughed. "I have staked my claim."

The Thal of Clan Sivio rose suddenly. "Then will you permit him to breed to me, sister? Your briski are bred, but I have two more to give my people."

Jael's lips parted, but before she could speak, Max stepped forward. He had just seen the answer to two problems. He took the younger Thal's hand. "Unfortunately, neither Jael nor I can give you your desire. I am sure Jael would be generous enough to agree, and I would consider it a great honor to father a briska for your clan, but I can father no briski on this world. I am no Bolvan—which Xers and Ptar know. Look at me carefully." He lifted his braided hair and kicked off his shoes and finally dropped his kilt.

When the gasps and hisses had died down, Max belted his kilt around his waist again and continued. "I am an offworlder. When I first came here the Zeli of Clan Vinci asked me why I had been sent to this world, and I had to answer that I did not know. But I believe I have found the answer now. The creature Bithe is also an offworlder—perhaps some renegade. Although it is not of my world, one offworlder can smell out another and can recognize the ugly toys he plays with."

Max stooped and picked up the leather-wrapped bundle he had brought to the council. He was conscious of Jael's eyes on him, but he did not glance at her. He had planted his seed of information (or misinformation) and he would reinforce it by displaying a familiarity with the blaster. By the time contact with Bithe was established, the idea that he was an offworlder would be fixed; the clans would not even raise the question of Old Ones. He folded back the wrappings to display the blaster and he explained what it was and what it did in great detail.

"This is a great danger," he concluded. "If Bithe has brought many others and has armed the Bolvi with them, no ordinary method of warfare can be successful. The clans must retreat and plan a whole new way of reaching Sinkek." He let that sink in for a moment, then said. "I have told you all that I know. Now it is for you to decide what you wish to do."

Tarbe moved impatiently. "We cannot decide this. It must be put to the test. Let us say that if most of the Bolvi are armed with this abomination we will flee to the mountains and take new counsel. If none or only a few are so armed, we will follow through our attack."

"I say also," the other Zeli and the Thals murmured. The motion was carried and the nampu scribbled away.

The next stage was the actual plan of attack. Max drew a map of the city roughly when asked, but it was quite apparent that, although they may not ever have attacked a city before, the Zeli understood diversionary tactics. Max, unwilling to interfere where it was not absolutely necessary, wandered over to the nampu. Quelv suspended her recording and looked up at him.

"When we are free of this burden," she quavered with determination, "you will find time to tell us of the past of your world. This, too, must be added to the scrolls."

Max suffered a momentary qualm of horror when he thought of the bloody history of Terra. Then he laughed. After the history of the Old Ones that could be read by anyone only a few bibars away in the dead city, Terra's troubles would seem like children's games.

"I will tell you all I can remember gladly, but tell me—why do you keep the scrolls?"

Quelv's eyes glittered for a moment with a passion that renewed their youth. "Only beasts do not record history. When we were beasts, the Old Ones kept the scrolls. Now that we are people, we keep them. How else could we see where we have been and, perhaps, by much study, see a little where we are going?"

Nodding agreement, Max nonetheless sighed. He hoped these people might learn more from their scrolls than Terra had learned from her history books. Then he wandered from nampu to nampu, observing that each kept a slightly different record. He was wondering what technique was used to unify the record, if any, when he felt eyes on him. He looked up to find all five Zeli and both Thals staring at him.

"Is there something you want me to do?" Max asked.

Jael laughed. "You have not been listening?"

"No," Max admitted.

"Since it is impossible for one body to obey seven heads—and the clans must act as one body—we have been discussing who shall lead us."

"I am willing to obey anyone the Zeli appoint,"

Max stated firmly and wondered why Jael laughed unroariously again.

"Out of his own mouth it is spoken," Tarbe said decisively, although he too was grinning. "I say Max shall be *Dux Bellorum.*"

Of course he did not use those Latin words—it took him a whole phrase to describe Max's position. Not as much as Dictator but more than General, a *Dux Bellorum* was a leader chosen in a time of war to unify disparate forces for a great effort.

"I say also," the two younger Zeli of Clan Sivio echoed, and their Thal murmured her agreement.

"I say," Xers shouted, grinning and proud of his protégé.

"I say," Ptar repeated, soberly.

"Who? Me?" Max gasped, recoiling. "But I am an offworlder."

"For that very reason," Jael pointed out.

Although Max's initial reaction was terror at the weight of responsibility thrust upon him, he could see the reasoning behind it and see that the idea was rational. And something inside him, whether a basic desire or preconditioning, did not permit him to protest. He looked from one face to the other, saw conviction.

"I will serve as well as I can for as long as the Zeli wish." He followed acceptance with an immediate order for the nampu to search the scrolls, even the records of the Old Ones, for similar cases. "For nothing since the first creation," he said, "is new."

By the time the related cases were brought to him, Max had worked out that ordinary clan procedures would serve his purpose. He would propose what he wished to the Zeli. If they agreed, they would carry the orders to the pevi. Thus, a few weeks later, Max was perched on a hillside feeling like Genghis Khan. In his tame technological paradise he had read of the migrations of the horde, but he had never even dreamed he would be looking down upon a rolling river of people flowing through a mountain pass.

The first stage of the plan was complete. Now the horde would divide into small groups to travel secretly by night through the more frequented mountain areas and the populated plains. At this last camp, the nampu and their scrolls and all the briski would remain. The fighting pevi would regather at the farm Max and Jael had robbed. It was ideal, being only a few bell-tenths' walking distance from the city but well out of sight behind a ridge. A few Enthok could stay to control the farm personnel. Max grinned as he thought of the groans of those chosen by lot (with the lots fixed, he was determined, so that the youngest Zel of Sivio got one) to stay behind.

The plan of attack was simple. Clan Sivio would attack the gates; Clan Vinci would climb the wall. Max's reasoning—those most recently injured would have the more immediate revenge, and those with the larger numbers would do the task most suited to a strong force—had been accepted without argument. The wall scalers would begin their attempt at midnight bell, which, sounded from the wall watch towers, would be clearly heard by all. What was more, midnight bell was the change of the watch, at which time there was always a lessening of attention and some confusion. Scouts of Clan Sivio would watch the wall scalers. If they were discovered, the attack on the gates would begin at once.

The two gates nearest the palace would be attacked first. When most of the Bolvi had been drawn there, a full-scale attack would be launched at the main gate. Meanwhile, a tiny group would feint at the single gate

on the sea side—no more than noise and a few arrows
—to keep the defenders from deserting their posts to
help the others. It was not important to force the gates,
Max emphasized, hoping to spare the city and the
Enthok unnecessary bloodshed. It was only important
to keep the Bolvi too busy to go to the aid of those
regularly stationed in the palace.

Aside from these plans and some advice on the tactics the Bolvi had been taught, Max did not interfere
with the normal battle techniques of the Enthok. This
had lost him Ptar because, foiled in her attempt to get
Max, the Thal of Sivio had opted for the senior Zel of
Vinci as father to her next briska. Ptar would fight with
Clan Sivio, the Enthok having discovered independently
the truth of Socrates' remark that nothing improves the
courage of a fighter like a lover's presence. Mates were
always battle companions. So Jael would climb and
fight beside him, precious Jael who was no longer a
silver goddess but a loving woman with sweet, warm
lips and an eagerly responsive body.

But now it was too late to fear. Max made himself
smile at Rib, whose silver eyes were incandescent with
excitement in his blackened face. Jael too looked at
her briska. Her lips twitched between fear and amusement. "Rib, you mind your place. It is your duty to
learn a Zel's duty from Xers. Do not shame me or your
father, who is not only a brave pev but a wise one."

"Yes, mother."

But the junior Zel danced away with an eagerness
that boded his safety little good. Max opened his
mouth and then shut it again. He and Jael had argued
Rib's role more than once in the privacy of their tent
but Jael, although she confessed that the mother's heart
in her was sick with fear, was immovable. Now it was
too late for fear, Max told himself again. The spear-

head of the wall scalers was assembling. Zabulin, blackened like the others, was ready and Xers with Helvig, now firmly gripping Rib's arm, arrived. Xers carried a strong bow—he was the best archer in the clan—a special arrow, with no point but a long, strong steel shaft, and a long light rope.

Max shouldered his pack of leather ladders, looked once more around, gave the signal to start, and began to climb the ridge. Twice he looked back. There was not a sound, not even of breathing. Not a shadow flickered on the long hillside. Yet there were hundreds of pevi following him. As the top of the ridge came in sight, Max crouched, then crawled. Belly flat, he came over the rise, inched over, crawled downhill. When he was far enough below the crest that he would not show up as a silhouette against the bright night sky, Max stood up and looked back again. Nothing. It was impossible. Then he heard a single pebble roll and, where the black ridge met the faintly luminous sky, there was a quiver of movement. Max went down, on through the windbreak of trees.

His legs were aching when he came to the fields that lay outside the city walls. Here the danger was greatest. The land was level and no brush or trees grew. Max crouched and looked back. Shadows moved across the fields, but at a few tens of bars they blended, rippling and then disappearing. At the edge of the fields he crouched again. Jael and Zabulin were beside him in moments and on their heels two larger and one small shadow. Max pointed out as well as he could the section of wall Jael had descended. Then they moved forward in irregular zigzagging rushes, dropping flat at each halt. The remainder of the clan would come more slowly, inching forward, covered with their dark cloaks to avoid notice.

Xers studied the wall silently and finally uttered a soft hiss of satisfaction when he spotted the tiny white bar of the candle marking the arrow slit. He drew a deep breath, crawled to the best position, and rose to his feet. Not even he could shoot a bow lying down. Max's body jerked involuntarily when the clink of steel against stone came faintly. Xers's first shot had missed. Silence again. Then another clink. Max bit his lip. Clink. Silence. Clink. Silence. Silence.

Max was so intent upon sound that he did not see Xers move and the hissing whisper made him jump again. "I have pulled the rope and it seems firm," Xers said. "Come, Rib."

The small shadow, looking humpbacked with the leather ladder strapped in a roll to its back, rose at once and ran forward. Max's heart jumped and began to pound. It was insane. If the rope should break or the arrow not be well seated, the briska could fall to his death. Max ran forward, signaling the others to come with him. At least they could stand under the rope. If Rib fell, perhaps one of them could break his fall. The silence lengthened. Max took Jael's hand in his and she gripped it fiercely. How long could it take to climb a rope twenty bars in length? Could the child have frozen with fear, be clinging, paralyzed, unable to move up or down? And then the ladder Rib had carried came tumbling down. Shaking with relief, Max started up it.

He hugged the excited briska just once before he ran to try the door. When it opened readily, Max's heart finally stopped leaping up and down in his throat. With Rib's help the other three ladders he had carried were soon fixed in place. Helvig arrived with another three and Rib went to help her as Max gave a hand to

Zabulin to speed him over the edge. The young Drail's eyes were wide with excitement, but, although he was carrying a considerable pack of supplies, he was not panting with exertion or trembling with fright. Zabulin's sojourn among the Enthok had done him a great deal of good.

Jael's head appeared as Xers swung himself over. She too hugged Rib, holding him for a moment and then slapping his shoulder gently as she broke the embrace. Max could see all the ladders straining against their ties now as the pevi started to climb. He would have to be quick. He turned to Zabulin.

"Are you still firm in your resolve?"

Perhaps the green skin yellowed a little, but Max could not see that under the blackening, and Zabulin nodded firmly. He touched Jael and gestured and she signaled understanding. Max led Zabulin out the door leading to the corridor over the Old Hall. He paused briefly to light one of the candles with which pev had been provided, then passed swiftly down the corridor to the chamber of the double doors. Strangely, he felt no reluctance to remove bars and wedges this time. Perhaps because this entry would relieve a burden on his conscience.

Max swung the outer door open, set his hand on the inner latch. Clearly, even under the blackening, Zabulin was yellow rather than green now. "If you do not wish to do this, hide elsewhere," Max murmured without contempt. He remembered that he had not been immune to the presence in that room. "I must go in."

"I do not swear that I will stay," Zabulin whispered, "but I wish to enter at least."

They did not pause in the outer chamber. At the door of the bedchamber where the thing lay, without

171

the slightest feeling of self-consciousness, Max bowed. "I have come to return that which I borrowed from you," he said to the empty eyesockets that stared at him. "I used only one small stone, and that was to pay a debt to your people."

He walked to the rifled dressing table, removed a package from his pouch, and returned the jewels he had taken. There was an old sensation of relief, as if a trust that had been placed in him had been fulfilled. Whatever lay there had set no value on the gauds he had taken, Max knew, but it had set a value on him.

Zabulin had remained at the doorway, staring, although little could be seen in the flickering light of the single candle beyond the black pits of the eyesockets in their frame of bone. As Max returned and passed him, he shuddered and pulled at the door. "The last Old One. No one has looked on his like—" Another shudder shook him, so strong that his hand jerked the door, which, far from being stiff with disuse, slammed shut with an enormous crash.

"Old One!" Max exclaimed, after the frozen shock of the crash had dissipated a little. "That was an Old One?"

Zabulin swallowed, but he replied steadily enough. "By the legends of the barred and wedged door above the Old Hall—yes. The last Old One—so far as our records know—on the whole of Gorona."

The aura of the room came back to Max. "That was no enemy of your people—nor regarded as one. Love laid out that body, tied those jaws, and left all intact."

"Or awe. No, it was no enemy, but it was a Master. We—at least I—would not welcome back even a kind Master."

"Nor would I," Max agreed heartily. He moved back to the door. "But it would not mind, I think, if I looked more closely upon it. I would like to know what kind of being an Old One was."

Perhaps it would not have minded, but the empty eyesockets no longer watched for incomers at the door. The shock had completed the work of the ages. A crumpled darker dust only lay upon the dust that had been a pillow. Max shrugged. Perhaps it was just as well. "He is gone for good," Max remarked, gesturing.

Zabulin looked, nodded, and closed the door again, gently this time. "I will wait here," he said. "When the time is right, I will come forth and raise my claim to be Zel, saying I took refuge with the Old One since my escape." He reached out to grip Max's elbow. "They may not accept me, but if I am successful Salf will be open to the Enthok for trade or for haven as long as I or any descendant of mine rules here."

"May you and yours reign long," Max said, "but I will say this to you out of the lore of my world. If you do not break custom and mate outside the royal family, your descendants will not hold Salf. To breed sib to sib of any close degree is not healthy."

"I have seen," Zabulin said dryly. "Also, I will not make my young so precious that I will wall them up. They will be free—as all young must be. It is better to have more briski, and complicate the succession, than to have—Sinkek and Delvinia."

Max acknowledged that with no more than a hand raised in salute and farewell. He had done what he could to ensure both Zabulin's safety and the safety of the raiding party. Zabulin could not be accused of treachery—and, indeed, had committed none; he had not offered, nor had he been asked for, information about his city. Moreover, with the excuse that he had never been out of the city, he would not be tempted to admit, and excuse, his connection with the raiding Enthok by giving warning of their invasion.

Chapter 15

Max returned at just the right moment. The pevi had made better time up the ladders than he expected and they were ranged in the corridor, candles ready lit, looking uneasily at the walls that hemmed them in. Max hoped that none would develop an acute attack of claustrophobia before they came to grips with the Bolvi and were too busy to think about such things. Jael was trying to describe the warren of corridors, but Max could see Xers shaking his head, an expression of disbelief and frustration on his face. Max's heart sank.

One part of his plan must be swiftly altered. It was clear that neither maps nor explanations would permit Xers to lead a way through the palace. Max would have to lead one group while Jael took the other if they hoped to bottle up Sinkek. Once he escaped into the maze that was the palace of Salf, there would be no way of trapping him. And if he got out into the city . . . No, not even to keep Jael by his side where he could protect her could Max take that chance. It would mean subduing the whole city and searching it stone by stone. Even that would be no guarantee of success because there was another door open to Sinkek—he could escape by the water gates to the sea.

Max touched Jael and she turned to him, but he spoke to the group at large. "We will do as the Thal advised from the first. In emergencies even battle customs must bend a little. Jael shall guide one party through these upper corridors. I shall lead another through the lower Halls. Thus we will block all the lair-openings of this urgel." Then, in defiance of the custom that kept gestures of love private, Max took Jael into his arms and kissed her long and hard. "For love of *me*," he muttered, "have a care of yourself."

There was some soft laughter and a few finger snaps of approval, but when Max started forward swords were ready drawn and the pevi filed silently behind him until Xers's gesture broke the group in half. The moons were just setting and the Hall of the Red Eyes of Trolg was a black cavern. The pevi, who had been told of the doors behind the tapestries, cursed when they realized the true extent of the problem. Anyone could come down any stair, invisible in the dark, and hide behind the myriad of pillars, while the light of the candles they needed to see the enemy would make them even more vulnerable. Bolvi could pour through any of the entrances to the Great Halls, make their way through them, and launch an attack on their rear.

"I do not think there is much to fear from the servant Bralidom," Max commented, "but ten shall go and bind those in the kitchens so that they cannot give warning or cause confusion. Another ten shall jam the locks in the four great Halls on this side of the palace.

This will not stop a determined group long, for the locks can be broken free of the doors, but the noise will give warning. Of the twenty who remain for these duties, five each, when the first task is done, will stay in each great Hall to capture any who would escape or seek help through those paths."

When the twenty had been chosen, Max led the remaining men into the Triumphal Hall. Here he left another twenty stationed at the guards' entrance. It was too small a force, really, but he hoped the Bolvi would be busy at the gates and, if the pevi fought right at the door, only two or three Bolvi could front them at any one time. Although Max made this suggestion and pointed out the danger of their force being over-whelmed, thus leaving the Enthok above open to an attack from the rear, he had little confidence his suggestion would be taken. Doubtless blocking the Bolvi would offend the Enthok sense of fair play—and interfere with their fun.

Max shrugged his shoulders philosophically. He had done, he believed, all that he could, and tenseness was rising in him. "There is a cloth over the door on the exit above. Let three or four burst through to hold the opening against the Bolvi and then one cut the cloth away so that the others may not be hindered."

It was the last order Max needed to give. Now, free of the burden of leadership, he ran to the stair, knowing a few pevi were following him while other groups made for other stairways. Although Jael and Xers knew the arrangements he had to make, it seemed to Max that he had taken far too long. He was dreadfully aware that Jael's group might have reached the outer inhabited regions by now, and if his men did not draw off some of the Bolvi things might go hard for them.

But now his hand was on the door. The latch clicked. The door swung inward.

Below, a voice of authority was raised in shock. "Get out of the— Who are you? Ware! Arms! Aid! Aid!"

Max had time for one bitter oath before he leaped sidelong past the tapestry, which was just as well because he barely avoided a thrust aimed directly at it. Although the corridors were much broken by cross links, enough unusual noise had reached the guards to make them uneasy. The pev behind Max struck the sword aside as it passed through the cloth, but the alarm had been raised.

Before Max could strike down that guard, others came running from the short end of the corridor where Sinkek's chambers lay—too many others. Max struck one, struck another. Then Chelve was on his right, his long sword flashing acceptance of a Bolvan challenge and Max dared spare time for a single glance over his shoulder. Doors were opening and more Bolvi were coming from the nobles' chambers.

A trap? Laid by whom? It did not matter because it was pure bad luck. From the expressions of astonishment on the faces of the Bolvi, the last people they expected to see were Enthok. Max cursed again, realizing they had somehow intruded into a palace revolution. He was momentarily distracted by wondering whether it was Delvinia's or Zabulin's friends and received the reward usually accorded those who let their minds wander during battle. Pain lanced along his ribs! That was why Jael's group had not yet reached this area. There must have been Bolvi in all the inhabited corridors—even those not usually guarded.

The trickle of warmth down Max's side warned him this was no time for divided concentration, but he was learning firsthand how wise Socrates and the Greeks

178

of his period were. Fear for Jael would not relax its grip on his vitals. He kicked—and missed. Hissing, Arile blocked the thrust that came at him. Max drew his sword. There was no room in the corridor now for hand fighting. There was no room to leap and dodge. He struck, thrust, shuddered involuntarily as a red spurt and a choked cry marked his success. Never in his life had any weapon Max used drawn blood.

Fortunately, the number of Bolvi was proving as much of a hindrance to their own party as to Max's. What with the pressure of Enthok pushing up the stair, the fighters were breast to breast. Sword locked against sword, Max neck-chopped the pev opposite him with his left hand. In the same moment, Arile, to his left, slid her dagger into the belly of the Bolvan she fronted. Both advanced the width of a body.

Under Max's raised sword arm, Holthank's blade spitted another antagonist. Chelve had been backed into the corridor wall, momentarily helpless. With the fall of Holthank's victim, Max had room to thrust. His blade drank again. Chelve lived—and Max scarcely noticed that another being had been injured, or even killed, for that purpose. Perhaps his society's inhibitions had never taken proper hold on him; perhaps there was an atavistic cruelty in him. It was enough that Chelve lived. There was no more room for guilt.

Chelve thrust strongly as soon as his sword arm was released, striving to retain the small freedom Max had given him. The Bolvan being pushed onto the sword without a chance to parry by the press of pevi behind him swung sideways desperately, and Max was able to remove another from the battle without drawing blood. The pev fell like a block, carrying with him Arile's opponent. With a shriek of laughter, the female leaped onto the two bodies. The elevation acquired, despite the uneasy footing enabled Arile to brain one Bolvan and disable another with a blow that broke his collarbone.

Max charged into the space created, delaying the Bolvan who was about to contest the piece of corridor with him with a kick to the groin. It landed solidly and would have disabled a human man, but the blow had little real effect on the pev. Max hissed with irritation. He had again forgotten that the males of Gorona kept the more delicate portions of their anatomy in a safer place than *Homo* did. The blow distracted the Bolvan sufficiently, however, for Holthank to strike his wrist so that the sword dropped from his hand. Max promptly felled him before worse could happen at Holthank's hands.

Taking a cue from Arile, Max mounted the body of the unconscious pev just in time to see the whole rear rank of Bolvi, several deep, turn away from the fighting and rush back around the corner of the corridor. That was incredible. Bolvi did not run from a fight unless, perhaps, all hope was really gone. Stupid, Max thought, as he leaped down to more secure footing while he fended off a rather skillful attack—even in that case they would not run away; they would cry "quarter." They must have been recalled.

Chelve and Arile had coalesced, and their efficiency increased geometrically. They had been battle partners for some time and knew instinctively what moves to make. Their practiced thrust and parry, combined with the relaxation of pressure from behind, was making the Bolvi fall back a trifle. Max found time to be aware of the ache in his side, of the sting of several minor cuts he had taken without even knowing it, of a faint giddiness. The latter worried him a little, hinting of a growing danger from loss of blood.

It was not important now. There were Enthok enough to hold the corridor. Max knew he could pull back if he needed to rest, but his blood was up; there was a fierce pleasure in this group fighting that he had never tasted even in his best combat bouts. And, regrettably, he realized that the sight and smell of blood—even his own—were the spices that made the pleasure so piquant.

Then, quite suddenly, Max understood why the Bolvi had been called back. Jael! Jael had remembered a bolthole for Sinkek that he had forgotten. There must be a back exit from the Zel's apartments to the corridor that held the tower stair. Max uttered a furious and terrified oath and redoubled his efforts. Thus far, unless blasters were being used at the gates, there had been no sign of the weapons. But Bithe's quarters must be close to Sinkek's, if not directly within Sinkek's private maze, and Bithe would not have left itself weaponless when an attack was suspected.

Holthank gasped as a sword thrust laid open his upper arm and made him drop his weapon. For a moment Max covered them both, but a fresh Enthok— one whose name Max could not remember just now— slipped sidelong past Holthank to replace him. The injured pev slid back along the wall, holding his arm and uttering a litany of blasphemies. There was room to fight now. The Bolvi were giving back. Max was not deceived into believing them ready to yield. What they wanted was room to fight in, since they had not been able to block the Enthok from getting to this level. Probably they were backing toward the broad corridor, almost a Hall itself, outside Sinkek's audience chamber.

181

It was a mistake on the part of the Bolvi, who had been trained in fighting in narrow spaces—a result of overconfidence from dealing too much with Bralidom. Max's eyes gleamed and he slashed about quite madly with his sword to encourage the retreat. In the relatively open space the advantage would be all with the Enthok, who, with their pair and triplet fighting units, would be far more efficient than the individualistic Bolvi.

As soon as they rounded the corner of the corridor, filled with the light of the newly risen sun, it was apparent that Max's guess had been right. Sounds of battle drifted out through the open double doors. An arrow whined by Max's ear, and he cursed the crazy Bolvi, who cared so little for their own that they would chance missiles when both sides were locked in close combat. Furiously he dispatched the pev he fronted and charged forward.

The unknown Enthok, practiced in two-man fighting even though he was a very young pev and as yet unmated, clung to Max's left side. Chelve and Arile were also well forward into the Bolvi. It was odd to hear the female's high laughter in the midst of the clang of metal and the low Bolvan oaths. Arile laughed a lot. Max spat another blasphemy and thrust the next Bolvan he met through the shoulder, kicking him in the head as he went down to be sure he would stay down. No sense of guilt tightened his throat or checked his breathing. Jael's laughter was softer, but she was probably just as merry—if she was not fried to a crisp already.

Desperation has its own special effect. Although Max had no particular superiority in swordsmanship, he moved steadily through the less frantic Bolvi—and where he went his Enthok followed, saving him, although he did not realize it, from being surrounded and borne down by the weight of numbers. Down the corridor and into the audience chamber they went to meet a seething mass of Bolvi and Enthok, completely mixed in battling groups. Freed of opponents momentarily, Max checked and swept the room with his glance. The group had not been in battle above a few bell-thousandths. No one had yet fallen and many of the duels were almost tentative, as if the opponents were feeling each other out. If Jael was here, she was no more endangered than anyone else in the whirlwind center of a battle. But terror told Max not to hope for such simplicity. His Jael would be seeking the monster in its own lair.

Fear paralyzes some; these do not become Combat Masters. In others fear raises a heightened consciousness. Four doorways led off the audience chamber. The two nearest the entrance corridor Max discounted. Neither Sinkek nor Bithe would permit privacy to be compromised by guard standers or corridor sounds. From that single sweep of observation, Max could even guess which inner chamber housed which enemy. Sinkek would be right, in brightness and luxury, where great windows faced the exquisite gardens and the Bolvi guardhouses. Bithe would be left, where the light came dimly oozing into the courtyards past the ancient Halls. But would the cravens be crouched together or would each be shivering in his own hidey-hole?

And then Max knew. Sinkek, robbed of his guards and his power, might shiver with fear—not Bithe. And Sinkek might run to Bithe for protection, but that which brought a blaster to Gorona would never offer protection to a useless ally.

Even as the decision was made and Max swung his first blow in that direction, a single flash of yellow light blazed in the dim doorway. With a howl like a soul in torment, Max plunged across the battle-filled chamber, twisting and dodging. His rush left his Enthok companion behind, and he burst through the entrance with another shriek that could have raised the dead.

Something blackened beyond recognition lay in the middle of the floor. Just clear of the entrance to the left, a huddle of shadows was marked as an Enthok by a flicker of silver skin. Across the chamber, edging toward another doorway, was the cowled form that must be Bithe. Watching for imminent death clears the vision. Max was able to pick out the dull gleam that betrayed the snout of a blaster peeping from the black sleeve. He saw the weapon start to swing toward him. Another saw. The glitter of a thrown knife startled Bithe into indecision, even though the range was too long for the thrower to hope for success. The blaster spat, but wavering between two enemies it missed both.

On the instant, Max dashed right to widen the field still more and threw his knife too. And then the Dance with Death began. And if Bithe was more knowledgeable with blasters than the Bolvan had been, this time Max was not alone. An arrow arced above Bithe's head—too high because Xers did not dare aim straight for his enemy. Max's movements were too erratic to chance a pev's-height shot. The blaster swung toward the silver gleam of the Enthok. Max threw a footstool he had chanced upon in crouching. It struck Bithe's leg. The blaster spat again. The chair the footstool had stood near flamed and crumbled, but Max was not there. Another arrow arced. Max leaped forward onto a low table. Again the blaster swung toward the Enthok, and this time it did not waver.

Max launched himself, a human missile on a near

hopeless errand. Pain—such pain—seared his left side. It did not matter. The hatred that burned inside was hotter and more painful. There was a shrill shriek, more like metal on metal than an animal cry of fear, and Max's hands found their target. He gripped as they fell together; he gripped and wrenched. The shriek scaled upward, ear-piercing. A dry twig snapped; he wrenched again and again at the limp and silent thing. Something tugged at him. Max snarled.

"Max, stop! Stop!"

He froze, glared mad-eyed at the nuisance. Then his hands fell away from what he held while he drew a long, tremulous breath.

"What were you trying to do," Jael gasped, "tear its head off?"

Max moved his left arm gingerly. He was afraid to look, although the pain was diminishing. "I thought that—" he gestured toward the blackened remains— "was you."

Jael shuddered. "It was the other female, Sinkek's sib-mate. When we broke through into the large chamber, they ran here for protection, and it burned her down. Sinkek was to be next. It was just turning the blaster on him when Xers loosed an arrow. That startled it, and it started to run but I—I would not let it go. I cried aloud for Xers to shoot it in the back if need be."

Still on his knees, Max pulled Jael closer with his good arm and buried his face in her thighs. It was no fault of hers that she was not another crisped thing on the floor. She knew what a blaster could do. "Did I not tell you to have a care?" Max grated furiously. "To challenge a cornered urgel with a blaster—is that care?"

Suddenly her legs began to tremble. "I thought we

were dead. I knew he would die. But if it escaped . . ."
A little shaky laugh followed. "And then you came—
and we live."

Max lifted his head. Alive, so far, but the battle
continued. He climbed to his feet, wincing and biting
back a groan and forced himself to look down at his
left side. Pain, which had begun to score his nerves,
receded as fear of serious injury yielded to evidence.
Instead of the blackened and cracking flesh he had
expected, he saw a neatly cauterized gash across his
ribs and what looked like a really nasty sunburn.
Bithe's reaction time was slow. Most of the blast had
never reached him. Relief from personal terror, however, raised a new, equally serious problem.

"Where is Sinkek?" Max cried.

"I have him safe." The voice, still treble, was nonetheless firm. Rib prodded his prisoner forward with his
sword. Sinkek's hands were firmly tied and his feet
hobbled. Max grinned. Xers, Helvig, and Jael stared.

"Rib, you will make a mighty Zel," Xers said won-
deringly. "Anyone who could take time to tie up a
prisoner while all that was going on is a better pev
than I."

Jael shook her head, half proud, half disapproving.
"He is just like his father," she exclaimed. "Never
in my life did I know anyone more practical."

"Well, he certainly did not get any common sense
from you," Max remarked bitterly. Then he turned to
Xers. "Put a knife to his throat and get him to order
the Bolvi to stop fighting. If he will not, show him captive and cry truce with them. There is no need for
more pevi to die. Then find a Manili who will stop the
fighting at the gates.

Xers looked a little disappointed—for him the fighting had not really started—but he nodded agreement. Jael turned as if to follow, but Max caught her arm.

"Wait," he muttered. When the others had gone out, he knelt stiffly and threw back the hood that concealed the dead thing's face. Both stared, but Max's eyes were fixed with horror while Jael was merely shocked and revolted.

The skin was truly black, shiny smooth, like—Max recalled the description, thinking for a moment in Universum—a black rubber wetsuit. No hair. The eyes seemed lidless and they were very large, either all pupil or with very black irises. No nose. There should be breathing orifices in the neck, but Max could not bring himself to touch the creature again to prove the point. No lips. The mouth was a slack, round orifice, limp and dangling.

"That is no Old One!" Jael exclaimed when she had mastered her shock enough to speak.

Max forced his eyes away and swallowed the bitter gall rising in his throat. Now he knew why he had been sent—why Terra's administration, whose favorite motto was "Mind Your Own Business" had decided to interfere in the affairs of a distant planet. Terra was at peace with herself and with the Universe, but she had not forgotten her one vendetta. All through the slow-rolling centuries the search went on.

"Nompeg!" Max spat. Hatred swelled in him. However few remained, they had not changed. Had they lived quietly, without disturbing their environment, the searchers would never have found them. They could have lived in peace. But they still sought to eat other civilizations.

"Max, what is it?" Jael asked.

"Not your ancient fear, but mine," he growled. "The ancestors of this filth nearly destroyed my world."

"Ah!" Jael was pleased to have a puzzle solved. "That was why you were sent. It is good that it is dead." Her head turned toward the open door. The problem was eliminated and she lost interest in it.

The sound of fighting was dying down, and the soft cries and groans of the wounded were louder than the clash of weapons. Soon wounds would be bound and the Bolvi and Enthok would part quietly, without enmity—two tribes who had each done an honest job honestly. There would be no hatred, no reprisals, no postwar bloodbath. The creature who had nearly destroyed the balance was dead. His willing dupe and ally . . . Max was not sure of Sinkek's fate, but probably it would be a swift and clean death. Probably also Zabulin would be the next Zel of Salf, but any other would be better than Sinkek. And with Bithe's influence gone . . .

There was the one rub, the one fly in the ointment. Was Bithe the only one? The Nompeg were very few, but was Bithe the only spot of infection in this world? Having been cleansed, would the body of Gorona remain healthy? Bithe was said to come out of Elven . . . Deep inside Max felt a stirring of purpose again, but he was too tired just now. The flame of his hatred died to a small hot core. He covered the dead countenance, rose, and took Jael into his arms.

" 'Take therefore no thought for the morrow.' " he muttered, " 'for the morrow shall take thought for the things of itself. Sufficient unto the day is the evil thereof.' "

Glossary

arbas (sing. and pl.): the abandoned cities of the Old Ones, many ruined and radioactive

bar (pl. **bars**): a unit of measure equal to about 0.5 m. (1.5 ft.)

bibar: a unit of measure, bi = 1000; therefore bibar = 500 m.

Bolvan (pl. **Bolvi**): a race of humanoid reptiles characterized by brown skin and eyes and black "hair." They live in lone family groups, many females dominated by one male; at puberty the sons are driven out.

Bralidom (sing. and pl.): a race of humanoid reptiles characterized by green skin (in many shades), gold eyes, and gold "hair." These are the most civilized; they live in city-states (like the Greeks) and have about the same level of technology except that they can work steel as well as brass and bronze.

189

briska (pl. **briski**): a male or female child

cebar: a unit of measure, ce = 1/1000; therefore cebar = 0.5 mm (0.13 in.)

Drail (sing and pl.): a member of the royal family of a Bralidom city

elef: money, a silver coin

Enthok (sing. and pl.): a race of humanoid reptiles characterized by silver skin, eyes, and "hair." These people are nomadic hunters who increase their "income" by serving as mercenaries in the wars between the city-states. They are ruled by three or four male Zeli and a female Thal. The duty of the female (aside from helping to rule) is to provide the future rulers by mating with (at least) four *different* males who may come from inside or outside the clan and even from a different race, if the Thal so chooses.

fibbil: a fruit, something like an apple

gibbous lob: a mammal, small, furry, arboreal, kept as a pet by the reptilian races of the planet

gobari (sing. and pl.): a reptile very much like a pig, the most common prey of the Enthok in the wild, domesticated by the Bralidom

Gorona: "Earth"; that is, the name of the planet

nampu (sing. and pl.): an elder, seer, adult too old to fight, record-keeper

pev (pl. **pevi**): an adult person, male or female, a warrior

Thal: royal sister, the breeder of the next generation of rulers of the tribe or clan

Trolg: god of death and justice; ruler of the many heavens and hells

Zel (pl. Zeli): tribal chief, leader of battle, ruler

Yelth: goddess of luck (good and bad), life, and mercy

Great SF Authors

Great Science Fiction from Pocket Books